RAZOR-SHARP DEATH

Snarling in rage, Raider caught his balance, whirled around and charged across the tepee in Loncey's direction. Seeing the man approaching with a raised tomahawk, the boy acted without any conscious thought. Instinct fostered by generations of knife-fighting men caused him to whip back his arm and swing it forward, the knife leaving his hand as it had so many times in practice.

Flying steel and charging man converged. An instant too late Raider realized what had happened. He felt the knife's point prick his throat, then its blade sliced home. Dying on his feet, the man let his tomahawk drop, clawed at the knife's hilt in his blood-spurting flesh, and crashed to the ground.

Books by J. T. Edson

THE NIGHT HAWK
NO FINGER ON THE TRIGGER
THE BAD BUNCH
SLIP GUN
TROUBLED RANGE
THE FASTEST GUN IN TEXAS
THE HIDE AND TALLOW MEN
THE JUSTICE OF COMPANY Z
McGRAW'S INHERITANCE
RAPIDO CLINT
THE BLOODY BORDER

Comanche

J. T. EDSON

A DELL BOOK

Published by
Dell Publishing
a division of
Bantam Doubleday Dell Publishing Group, Inc.
666 Fifth Avenue
New York, New York 10103

ISBN: 0-440-20930-7

Printed in the United States of America

Published simultaneously in Canada

June 1991

10 9 8 7 6 5 4 3 2 1

OPM

1

Sam Ysabel's Gain and Loss

The village of the *Pehnane,* Wasp, band of the Comanche Nation scattered for almost a mile along the Mustang Fork of the upper Pecos River, an area ideally suited to their needs. Numerous canyons, arroyos and valleys in the open timber country offered shelter and protection for the village, along with adequate grazing for its sizable horse herds. There also could be found a plentiful supply of buffalo. At the right time of the year, the bugling of mate-hunting wa-piti mingled with the sudden rushing crash as whitetail deer fled from some suspicious sound; for this was Texas in 1847, before the cattleman came with his long horned "spotted buffalo" or the settler moved in with his towns and long, long before the oilman came to scar the land with iron monstrosities in search of "black gold."

Centuries of nomadic experience had taught the Comanches how to settle in a new location at frequent intervals, without disturbing the even flow of their lives. On arrival at

a new camping ground, the village arose without fuss or
argument. The members of each war lodge tended to gather
in a group about the tepees of its senior chief, but beyond
that nobody objected to who set up house as a neighbor. The
village came, rose and continued its normal activities almost
as if it had been there since the world began.

Busy women and unmarried maidens went about their
daily tasks of preparing and cooking food, scraping or tan-
ning hides for later use, making and repairing clothing or
tepees. Old men, aided by their Mexican prisoner-appren-
tices, built saddles, produced bows or arrows to be bartered
to the warriors who had not time to make their own, being
engaged in men's work. Such of the braves who were not
away on hunting or raiding expeditions gathered in groups
to gamble or talk, sat cleaning and sharpening weapons,
trained a favorite horse, or merely lazed away the time while
awaiting the arrival of a meal.

It was a normal sort of day, with the ordinary functions of
Comanche life taking place. Yet to one man it had become
the most important day of his life. In a tepee to the rear of,
and away from, the rest of her family's cluster of dwellings
his wife went through the hell of bearing their first child.

Much as he wished to, Sam Ysabel knew he could not
show too close an interest in the proceedings taking place
inside the birth tepee. He might be a white man, but had
been accepted into the *Pehnane* and adopted as a member of
the Dog Soldier lodge and so must adhere to their ways and
traditions. No warrior would risk spoiling his war medicine
by approaching and entering a tepee in which childbirth was
about to happen.

So Ysabel squatted on his heels by the family fire, trying
to act unconcerned while making light conversation with his
father-in-law, Chief Long Walker. Some of Ysabel's tension
found light relief that Long Walker also showed much interest in the birth tepee, although the chief tried to hide it as
did the big white man. Both hoped for a son to be born.
While a girl would be accepted and given loving care, every

father secretly hoped his firstborn was a son to carry on the family line. Long Walker also hoped for a boy, someone to whom he could pass on the knowledge gained in a lifetime of achievement; for it fell mainly on the grandfather to instruct the male child while the father went about the man's work of hunting, raiding and making war.

Ysabel rose to his feet in a swift, effortless swing, turning to look around the village. Despite his name, he was not Mexican but as Irish as a four-leaved shamrock. Something over six feet in height, he towered over the average Comanches, who tended to be of medium size and stocky. Bareheaded, his shoulder-long hair framed a face tanned almost Indian dark. He wore a fringed buckskin shirt hanging outside trousers of the same material. The moccasins on his feet, made, as his clothes had been, by his wife, also sported the traditional Comanche decorative fringing. Around his waist, he wore a belt that supported a long-bladed James Black bowie knife in a decorative sheath, but no handgun. So far only a comparative few revolvers had made their appearance in Texas and Sam Ysabel regarded the .36 caliber Paterson Colt as being too light for consideration as a serious weapon. Of course one heard rumors that Yankee, Colt, aimed to bring out a real powerful handgun on the lines suggested by Captain Sam Walker of the Texas Rangers. Happen he followed Cap'n Sam's advice, he ought to turn out something worthwhile. When such a gun came along, Ysabel would make his decision on its merits. Born of black-Irish Kentuckian stock, he regarded the rifle as the ultimate weapon and pistols as toys for the effete gentry's use.

Among the Comanche in general, and the *Pehnane* in particular, Ysabel had built himself a name as a bone-tough fighting man and bad medicine to cross. No mean achievement in a nation of warriors and when living as a member of the toughest, proudest of all the *Pehnane* war lodges. Certainly Long Walker had no cause to regret allowing the only child of his French Creole *pairaivo*, senior wife, marry the big white man. Riding as a scout for the U.S. Army against

the Mexicans, he brought back much loot. Few of the
Pehnane braves could equal Ysabel's skill as a hunter and
none even approached him in the accurate use of a rifle. One
way and another, Ysabel proved himself to be all that a
senior war chief might desire as a son-in-law.

"I hope this don't take long," Ysabel said, speaking English although he knew the Comanches' language as well as
his own. Then, remembering where he was, went on so the
chief might understand him, "I told Cap'n Walker I'd be
back in a week at most when I got word that Raven Head
was near her time."

"These things can't be rushed," answered Long Walker
philosophically, sucking at the stone pipe loaded with a gift
of white man's tobacco.

For such an important occasion as the birth of his first
grandchild, the chief naturally wore his best clothing.
V-necked, long-fringed, decorated with beads, porcupine
quills and the scalps of three enemies who had fought well
enough to deserve the honor, his buckskin shirt hung over a
breechclout colored blue, the traditional hue for wearing
upon such an important day. Close-fitting buckskin leggings
extended from each ankle to hip, fringed and decorated by
loving hands, and his moccasins bore a polecat's tail edging
instead of the common buckskin fringe. Dressed in such a
manner, with tomahawk and knife at his belt, Long Walker
figured he could perform his part in the forthcoming proceedings in a manner which did honor to the child soon to
arrive.

Although pretending to be laconic and interested in the
doings around the camp, Ysabel paid little attention to the
familiar scene. Anxiety ate at him for he loved the slender,
beautiful Raven Head and was all too aware of the high
mortality rate among Comanche women at childbirth. However, he knew that his wife received the best possible attention.

As became the daughter of an important chief and wife of
a wealthy, successful warrior, Raven Head did not lie in a

small lodge hastily built of brushwood. Despite the fact that it would have to be destroyed after much use, she was given a tepee in which to produce her child.

Inside the tepee all had been prepared. Underfoot the earth was made soft by digging and two pits prepared; in one a fire burned and kept boiling a cooking pot full of water, the other being used as a repository for the afterbirth. Raven Head lay on the single bed, hot rocks placed against the small of her back to speed the labor, sipping at the thick soup held to her lips by Raccoon Talker, the medicine woman in attendance. Two women hovered in the background, ready to render aid at Raccoon Talker's command, howling dolefully and singing mournful songs designed to prevent any of the mother-to-be's cries of pain reaching the ears of those beyond the tepee walls.

Suddenly Raven Head's body twisted in a spasm of pain far worse than any felt so far. Twisting her head away from the soup basin, she clutched wildly at the stout stakes sunk deep into the earth alongside the bed, clinging to it and fighting down a desire to scream. Wise in such matters, Raccoon Talker signaled the assistants forward and passed the basin to one of them. Then the medicine woman gave Raven Head her full attention.

Jumping like a coyote-startled jackrabbit, Ysabel spun around to face the tepee. After a momentary faltering, the women's prebirth chant resumed, but only for a short time. A thin, coyotelike wail rose faintly, to be drowned out by the opening words of a song of rejoicing. Shortly after Raccoon Talker emerged from the tepee. Carrying the baby's severed umbilical cord in her hand, she went to hang it among the branches of a nearby hackberry tree. The cord would be watched with interest during the following days. If it remained undisturbed until rotting away, the baby could look forward to a long, eventful, prosperous, and successful life.

Standing by the fire, Sam Ysabel fought to hold down his impatience. He wanted to know what had happened inside the tepee, but the appearances must be kept up. On no account would he allow his wife to be mocked at a later date because he broke the strict traditions of his adopted people.

After what seemed like a very long time, Raccoon Talker returned to the tepee. She disappeared inside, to appear a moment later carrying the afterbirth wrapped in a piece of skin and bore it away to be thrown into the purifying waters of the river well clear of the camp. Not until that had been done could Long Walker perform his part in the ritual.

"It is time, *naravuh,*" Ysabel said, trying to sound disinterested.

A grin came to Long Walker's lips at the familiar joking term for an old man, the first time it had been applied to him.

"So I am a *tsukup* now, am I?" he replied. "Well, maybe it is not so bad as it allows me to go and ask that which we both wish to know."

While walking toward the tepee, Long Walker wondered if becoming a grandfather really turned him into a *tsukup,* an old man. Certainly he did not feel old, but maybe the bravehearts would not care to be led on the war or raiding trail by a grandfather. Yet he had no wish to retire from active life. A known warrior might be called into consultation after becoming *tsukup,* but only in an advisory capacity and he could no longer command; that coyote-yip cry from the tepee meant it was too late to change things.

Halting outside the tepee, he called out his name and hoped he would not be answered by the words *"Esamop 'ma,"* meaning he had a granddaughter. The women in the hut only needed to hear his name to know that Long Walker performed a grandfather's duty by coming to inquire after the baby's sex.

"Eh'haitsma!" one called.

That was what Long Walker had hoped to hear. The words "It is your close friend" meant a boy had been born. Under Comanche tradition the maternal grandfather became very close to his grandson and it fell upon the man to see that the boy received correct training to fit him for his place in life.

Even before Long Walker turned to walk away, one of the women emerged and painted a large black dot on the tepee wall. The sign told all who wished to see that a son had been born and the strength of the *Pehnane* increased by another braveheart warrior. With that part of the ritual completed, the woman returned to the tepee's interior and lent a hand to complete the less dramatic, but more important, business of the birth.

Inside the tepee gentle hands washed the baby, applied antelope grass to his body, and then dusted it with a powder made from the pulverized dry rot of a cottonwood tree. After wrapping the squirming, squalling youngster in soft rabbit skins, one of the women carried him to the cradleboard which would form his home, bed and carriage during the first months of his life. Lifting the cradleboard and its tiny burden, she carried both to the bed and showed them to the wan-looking mother. Slowly Raven Head raised a hand to touch the baby's cheek. She smiled at her son and pointed weakly to the tepee's door. Nodding her understanding, the attendant took the baby out into the fresh air. Raven Head had made the cradleboard, showing the same loving care which went into all her work. Instead of the basket of rawhide fastened to a flat, angular board, she built a soft buckskin sheath that laced up the front and was firmly anchored to the backboard. In later days the board could be stood on its end out of harm's way, or carried upon its maker's back while she went about her work.

Waiting with what patience he could muster, Sam Ysabel thought of the future. In the background people began to gather, waiting until the formalities had been completed before moving up close. Ysabel knew he would have to present the first visitor to inquire about the happy event with a gift; a good horse at least if he hoped to retain his name as a noble, generous *Pehnane* warrior. Well, he could spare it. During his work against the Mexicans, he helped capture

the remounts of a Lancer Regiment and received thirty
horses for his trouble. Once the Mexican fuss came to an
end, Ysabel could return to the village and settle down for a
spell watching his son grow up.

At that moment the woman appeared at the tepee door.
Throwing aside all pretense of nonchalance, Ysabel strode
forward. On reaching the woman, he held out his hands,
accepting the cradleboard. With a gentleness that might
have surprised his comrades-in-arms, he held the board before him. His normally expressionless face softened into a
smile as he gazed down. A red, button-nosed face twisted
into a squall, with a wet mouth open as it wailed, looked up
at him.

"Is Raven Head well?" he asked.

"It is too early to say yet," the woman replied. "But you
have a fine son."

"That I have," agreed Ysabel and looked once more into
his son's red-hazel eyes. "Hello, Loncey Dalton Ysabel.
That's your name, boy. And don't you ever disgrace it."

As Ysabel said the last words in English, the woman
could not understand him. She put the speech down to being
some kind of prayer the white man made to whatever
strange Great Spirit he worshiped, asking support for the
newborn through its life. From her experience with Comanche fathers, she doubted if Ysabel would want to take up
any more time when he had entertaining to do. Retrieving
the cradleboard from the white man's reluctant fingers, she
turned to reenter the tepee.

Suddenly a cry rose from inside, halting the advance of
friends and relatives coming to celebrate the birth. The
sound drove into Sam Ysabel like a knife thrust, for it had
been that of a woman in mortal pain. At Ysabel's side, Long
Walker also heard, recognized his daughter's voice and
swung to face his son-in-law.

"Fetch Raccoon Talker back—quickly!" ordered the
chief.

Only for an instant did Ysabel hesitate. He had been on

the verge of plunging into the tepee, but Long Walker's words bit into him and halted his advance. Sick with anxiety, the white man whirled and raced to where his favorite horse stood picketed before the door of his tepee. At the time of approaching childbirth no Comanche brave could share his wife's tepee without endangering his war medicine and Ysabel went along with the convention. He cursed the delay caused by having to run that extra distance before starting to fetch back the medicine woman. Out came his bowie knife and he slashed through the picket rope. Without bothering to saddle the big grulla stallion, Ysabel bounded up on its back. Eager to be moving after several days of good feed and inactivity, the stallion sprang forward and went racing through the camp. People scattered before his rush, those close to the birth tepee realizing what caused it and the others wondering, or guessing, at Ysabel's reason for haste.

Tearing along the bank of the stream, Ysabel saw Raccoon Talker standing in a clearing after disposing of the afterbirth. The woman heard the drumming of hooves and turned to see who approached. Recognizing Ysabel, she sensed instantly what caused his rush. In her time as a medicine woman she had attended at many a childbirth and knew just how swiftly something could go wrong. Even an apparently trouble-free delivery might develop unforeseen complications of a serious nature. The sooner she returned to the birth tepee, the better she would be pleased.

Ysabel wasted no time in explanations, knowing there would be no need for them. From her actions, Raccoon Talker needed no words. Nor did she even expect him to delay by halting for her to mount the stallion. Sweeping up to the woman, Ysabel reached down and caught her offered wrist. Showing surprising agility for a stocky, middle-aged woman—unless one remembered that much of her life had been spent on the back of a horse—Raccoon Talker vaulted up behind the big white man. With the woman safely seated,

Ysabel brought the horse around in a turn and headed it back at a gallop in the direction of the village.

Once more the people scattered, staring at Ysabel tearing his grulla between the tepees with Raccoon Talker clinging precariously behind him. On approaching the front of the birth tepee, he brought the horse to a rump-scraping halt. Even before the animal stopped, Raccoon Talker slipped from its back and ran into the tepee. Leaping down, Ysabel started to follow the woman, but Long Walker caught his arm in a viselike grasp and halted him.

"You must not go in, Ysabel," the chief warned. "It is woman's work. You can do nothing and it might bring bad medicine for you to try."

Only by exercising all his willpower did Ysabel fight down his inclination to hurl the older man aside and burst into the tepee. Common sense though told him that he could do nothing, and might even make matters worse with his presence. Raven Head might have a French-Creole mother, but was born and raised a Comanche. She firmly believed in good and bad medicine and it might worsen her condition if she saw him breaking the beliefs of her people.

Swinging away from the tepee, he walked to his horse and halted at its side. Silence fell on the assembled crowd, every eye fixed on the closed door of the tepee. Almost fifteen minutes dragged by, the longest Sam Ysabel could ever remember. Then a wail, soul-tearing in its mournful context, rose from the tepee. A low cry broke from the lips of Raven Head's mother and her voice joined that which sounded from the tepee. Woman after woman took up the chant, doleful, wordless, but filled with misery and suffering. It was the death chant of the *Pehnane*.

Ysabel started toward the tepee, his face drawn into harsh savage lines. Lifting the flap, Raccoon Talker stepped out to meet the advancing man.

"What happened?" he demanded, hoping against hope.

"She— She is dead." Raccoon Talker answered, shoulders drooping. "It was something that I—"

Without waiting to hear more, Ysabel thrust by her and entered the tepee. He did not even glance at the two wailing women who hovered in the background as he flung himself to the bed. Dropping to his knees, he looked down at and barely recognized the agony-distorted, blood-smeared face of his wife. Gently he lifted the still shape, cradling it in his arms and holding it to him as if to try to return its life by some means.

Ysabel belonged to that free-ranging breed of pioneers who opened up the West and paved the way for the more permanent citizens to follow. Always wishing to see what lay beyond the next hill, avoiding as much as possible the ever-advancing flow of settlers, his type of man sought for new land where they might live away their rich, free lives. Coming to Texas originally with a party of wild-horse hunters, Ysabel found it to be a land which met all his requirements. To make a home beyond the fringe of Mexican-held towns called for the friendship of the Indians and Ysabel had succeeded in gaining acceptance among the Comanche, greatest tribe of all. Some of his kind took an Indian wife as a convenience, a means to cement their friendship, discarding her when her usefulness ended. Not so Ysabel. He loved Raven Head and aimed to stay true to her. That made his grief at her death all the worse.

An irritatingly persistent sound cut into Ysabel's grief and after a moment he recognized it for what it was. Lowering his wife's body to the bed, he rose and crossed to where the baby lay in its cradleboard. For a moment anger rose in Ysabel. Then he realized that he could not blame the baby for its mother's death. Raven Head would not even have wished him to start thinking such a thought. With his mother dead, some other means of feeding Loncey must be arranged. Ysabel ran his tongue tip across his dry lips and turned his eyes to Raccoon Talker.

"Care for the child," he said. "I'll send women to—her."

Among the Comanches to mention a dead person by name had always been regarded as a sign of disrespect and

Ysabel went along with the tradition. Strangely, it helped ease the pain and grief not to say Raven Head's name.

"I will do what I can," Raccoon Talker promised.

"See the horse herd guard, tell him to give you the pick of the packhorses I brought in."

With that, Ysabel walked from the tepee. The gift served to show Raccoon Talker that he did not hold her responsible for Raven Head's death. Having attended to the medicine woman, Ysabel knew he must find some means of feeding his son—and do it quickly.

2
Death for a Poor Loser

Already the women of the immediate family circle had begun their mourning. Wailing their grief all the time, they returned to their tepees where they stripped off their clothes and donned rags or skin aprons. The two women attending the childbirth did not belong to Long Walker's family and so could not prepare the body for burial. That task fell upon Raven Head's weeping mother and two younger sisters. Dressed in their mourning clothing, they made for the birth tepee to begin their work.

Showing typical respect, the crowd faded off in silence. Long Walker laid his hand on Ysabel's sleeve and turned a grief-scarred face to the big white man. Neither of them spoke, they did not need words to express their feelings. Not until the women entered the tepee did Ysabel break his silence.

"We have to do something about feeding the baby," he said.

"We do," agreed Long Walker. "But how—?"

"*Wepitapu'ni*'s second wife has a son almost weaned," Raccoon Talker put in, coming from the tepee. "He may let you put the baby to her."

"He might at that," drawled Ysabel. "Let's go see him, Long Walker."

Wepitapu'ni, War Club, belonged to the Dog Soldier lodge and most probably would be willing to help out a fellow member. So after telling one of the women to inform his wife of their intentions, Long Walker went with Ysabel to the man's group of tepees. Being a successful warrior, War Club no longer housed all his family under one roof. Instead he supplied each of his four wives with a tepee, an arrangement which greatly added to their prestige in the village and met with their hearty approval.

Rising from her place by the family's fire, War Club's *pairaivo* greeted the two men politely and made the customary offer of a meal. Although all the wives gathered by the fire, there did not appear to be any sign of their husband. Hearing the wailing from the other side of the camp, and knowing the event expected by Ysabel that day, the *pairaivo* could guess at the reason for the visit. Her eyes went to Many Brothers, the second wife.

"Where is *Wepitapu'ni*?" asked Long Walker after courteously refusing the offered meal.

"At the Owl lodge camp, playing 'Hands,' " the woman replied.

Although the ruler of the family in her husband's absence, the *pairaivo* did not have the authority to make such an important decision as needed by Ysabel, so the two men thanked her and returned to Long Walker's tepees. Collecting their horses—like the cowhands who would one day inherit their range, the Comanche never walked when they could ride—the two men set off toward that section of the village which housed the Owl lodge's members.

In a life that saw much violence and danger, the Comanche lost most of their fear of death. However, they still clung to the old belief that the dead should be buried as soon as possible. So Raven Head's mother and two younger sisters wasted no time and did not allow their continued mourning to prevent them making the necessary arrangements.

Working swiftly, so as to be done before stiffness set into the body, the women bathed the naked corpse. They had already collected Raven Head's favorite clothing in which to dress the corpse and several of her friends brought along small items of jewelry or decoration to be added to her final raiment. With the body covered, vermilion stain was used to coat the face and its eyes sealed over by application of red clay. Then the women bent Raven Head's legs with her knees up against her chest and bowed her head upon the knees, holding the position by binding the body with a rope. After that, they set the body on a blanket to await Ysabel's return. In the period of waiting, such of Raven Head's relations and friends who wished might enter the tepee and pay their last respects.

With the work attended to, Raven Head's mother covered her face with black paint, wailing, moaning and sobbing all the while. Showing equal grief, the dead girl's sisters gashed themselves upon the arms and legs, letting the blood flow unheeded. Outside the tepee women joined in the funeral dirges and from inside came the wailing of the newborn, motherless baby.

Once beyond the sound of mourning, a different kind of music reached Ysabel and Long Walker's ears. Passing through the Owl lodge camp, the two headed in the direction of the music. At any other time they would have enjoyed hearing the deep-throated chanting of male voices, knowing that it heralded a pleasant and, sometimes, profitable diversion. Some quarter of a mile from the tepees, in a clearing at the foot of a hollow, several warriors and *tsukup* gathered to watch, take part in, or gamble on a game of "Hands."

Leaving their horses with the others at the head of the hollow's slope, Ysabel and Long Walker made their way on

foot toward the crowd. From what they could see, their
arrival coincided with a crucial moment in the game. It also
became obvious that the man they wished to see took a
major part in the game and must not be interrupted right
then.

A dozen men sat facing each other in two lines. Silent
concentration showed on the faces of the men at the left as
they watched War Club, seated in the right-side line, go
through the time-honored ritual of the game.

Basically "Hands" was a very simple game, its object being for one team to win the twenty-one tally sticks placed
between them at the start. To win a stick, a player concealed
a pebble in either hand and one of the opposing team must
then guess which hand held it. Should the guesser prove
wrong, his side lost a stick and the winning team retained
possession of the pebble. If a correct guess was made, the
guesser's team received the stick and took over the pebble.
Each team bet, as did the spectators, upon the result of each
individual guess and also on which team won all the sticks
first. Being inveterate gamblers, the men present wagered
high and tension mounted as the number of sticks before one
team or the other grew or shrank depending on the result of
the guessing.

At the time Ysabel and Long Walker arrived, the fate of
that particular game hung in the balance. Already twenty of
the sticks lay before War Club's team and he had possession
of the stone. Singing the gambling song with full-throated
vigor, beating a rhythm with the palm of the hand on a
parfleche bag, or a stick upon the ground, the remainder of
the possessing team attempted to distract their opponents.
While his teammates sang and drummed, War Club made
gestures and passes with his hands in time to the music. His
aim was to confuse the guesser and prevent him from knowing in which palm the pebble finally came to rest.

Seated facing War Club, a scowling, surly-faced Owl lodge
brave called Bitter Root watched the moving hands with
savage concentration. The fate of the game hung balanced

upon Bitter Root's next guess. Already he labored under the disadvantage of having cost his side a stick by fumbling and dropping the pebble while passing it from hand to hand, thereby forfeiting the point. Since that time his side failed to guess correctly and regain possession of the pebble. With a considerable stake involved, Bitter Root had no intention of failing through lack of concentration and attention.

Suddenly the singing and drumming ended. Extending his clenched fists, knuckles upwards, in Bitter Root's direction, War Club requested that the other make a choice. Slowly Bitter Root raised his right hand, moved it toward War Club's fists. All the time, he watched the other man's face, searching for some hint as to which fist gripped the hidden pebble.

Much as Sam Ysabel wanted to discuss his business with War Club, he knew he must not interrupt the game. While Ysabel and War Club belonged to the same lodge, and had shared danger upon two raids into Mexico, the *Pehnane* would take serious offense at having his concentration spoiled. Yet the matter entailed some urgency, for the newly born Loncey needed food. Of course, if Bitter Root made the wrong selection there would be no need to worry. Should he pick correctly, the game might continue for a considerable time. All too well Ysabel knew how the fortunes of a game of "Hands" swung back and forward. While the uncertainty contributed a major portion of the game's fascination, Ysabel had no wish to be delayed as the play seesawed back and forth indefinitely. Knowing his explosive nature, Ysabel wondered if he could hold himself in check for much longer.

Having so much at stake, Bitter Root did not rush his decision. He never took his eyes from War Club's impassive face, trying to read some clue. At the same time Bitter Root gave rapid thought to War Club's previous handling of the pebble. If he could recognize a pattern in the other's earlier moves, it might help the decision. Yet, try as he might, Bitter Root failed to pick up any thread. An old hand at the game, War Club varied his selection, sometimes offering the

pebble in one hand on successive turns, on other occasions
changing hands. Nor did he allow his face to show emotion.
A keen-eyed guesser could read much in his opponent's face
and might notice a flicker of concern when moving his finger
as if to touch the hand holding the pebble.

Bitter Root's finger wavered between War Club's right
and left fist, but no decision was made until actual contact
be made. A man could learn much by pretending to have
reached a decision and moving the finger toward one fist.
Just a faint show of concern, or jubilation, could tell its
story. However, he could read nothing and his annoyance
grew.

Reaching a decision, Bitter Root laid his finger upon War
Club's right fist. Instantly a broad grin came to the Dog
Soldier's face and he opened his hand to show an empty
palm. As whoops of delight rose from his supporters,
mingling with Bitter Root's savage ejaculation and the
groans of those who bet on the losing team, War Club turned
over his left hand and exposed the pebble gripped in it.

Singing the special victory song, War Club's supporters
rose and prepared to gather their winnings from the stake-
holders. With the exception of Bitter Root, all the losers
took defeat in good part. Personal property, with certain
exceptions such as weapons or a prized horse, meant little to
a Comanche brave. If he lost, he could always go out raiding
and obtain more. Smarting under the stigma of being the
one responsible for the losses, Bitter Root took a less toler-
ant view of the matter. Never the most amiable of men, his
name having a firm foundation in his character, Bitter Root
looked for someone on whom he might vent his anger.

Accepting the congratulations from all sides, War Club
strolled to where Sam Ysabel and Long Walker passed
through the crowd.

"Are you joining the next game, Ysabel?" he asked, raising a hand in greeting. "We will be starting again soon."

"I'm not playing," Ysabel replied. "Can I talk with you
before you start, *Wepitapu'ni*?"

Suddenly War Club realized that this was the day that Raven Head expected her child. He also became aware of the grief lines on the two men's faces and could guess at its cause. Thinking quickly, War Club came up with one explanation for the men's presence, the right one as it proved.

"Of course," he said.

Before the three men could withdraw from the noisy crowd, Bitter Root came slouching in their direction.

"Hey you, War Club!" he called arrogantly. "We are about to play another game. What do you want me to bet against the four horses you won from me?"

"Make me an offer," answered War Club. "But first my lodge brother, Ysabel, wants words with me."

Such a statement given to most *Pehnane* braves would have been sufficient to cause a withdrawal until the other's private business was completed. By tradition a braveheart warrior should be polite, within certain bounds, generous and considerate of other members of the band. Bitter Root lacked those qualities. Instead of standing back and allowing War Club to speak with Ysabel, he remained close by, his surly face creased in a scowl. The four horses lost on the game of "Hands" formed his highly-prized war string, specially trained for the exacting business of long distance raiding, and he hated the thought of parting with them.

Ignoring Bitter Root, a man he cordially disliked, Sam Ysabel told War Club what he wanted. Without wasting any time, or giving a thought to how he might profit in the matter, War Club gave his agreement that Many Brothers act as wet nurse to the motherless baby.

"Come, brother," the Dog Soldier said. "We will go to my tepee and tell Many Brothers to prepare herself. Gray Foot, my *pairaivo,* will help her."

"You won't have any time to go and be back before the start of the next game," Bitter Root objected.

"Then I'll have to miss it," War Club snapped back, angry at the intrusion into a purely personal and private matter.

"You have to stay, play and give me a chance to win back my horses!" shouted Bitter Root, bringing every eye to him.

Among the Comanches, quitting while ahead carried no stigma of poor sportsmanship. So only Bitter Root's surly nature—and possibly a dislike of Sam Ysabel—caused his insistence on being given a chance to win back the horses. Although a low mutter of disapproval rose from the crowd at Bitter Root's shouted words, he ignored the condemnation. Being a name warrior, rich and successful by *Pehnane* standards, he cared little for public opinion and determined to enforce his will upon the other man.

Against a young brave, or a man about to become *tsukup*, Bitter Root's attitude might have caused compliance to his demands. However, War Club was also a known warrior, one of the recklessly brave men who carried the war lance into battle instead of using a bow. Such a man did not lightly yield to demands made in an offensive tone and manner. Swinging away from Bitter Root as if the man had not spoken, War Club looked at Sam Ysabel and Long Walker.

"Come, we will see my women."

An awful fury creased Bitter Root's face at the other's rejection. Snatching the knife from his belt, he gave a snarl of rage and lunged toward the two men. The snarl proved to be a bad mistake, for it gave warning to his intended victims. Wishing to avoid trouble, Sam Ysabel acted in the only manner possible. Fast as a striking rattlesnake, he pivoted around to meet Bitter Root's charge. Out swung Ysabel's left hand, striking Bitter Root's knife wrist and deflecting the blade. In a continuation of the same move, Ysabel lashed the back of the hand up and across the Indian's face. The blow did not land lightly and Ysabel packed considerable strength in his powerful frame. Bitter Root shot aside under the force of the blow, dropping his knife and crashing to the ground.

In an instant the man regained his feet. Although he had lost his knife, a tomahawk hung in its slings at his waist belt. Jerking the weapon free, Bitter Root gave a war screech and

rushed forward once more. Cold fury gripped Ysabel, turning him into that deadly efficient fighting and killing ma-
chine which so endeared him to the *Pehnane* braves. He
wanted no trouble, but was having it forced upon him. More
than that, Bitter Root's attack delayed the arrival of food for
Raven Head's hungry baby.

Trained fingers fanged down and slid the bowie knife from
its sheath. Even as the knife's long blade came clear, Ysabel
dropped to one knee. The tomahawk hissed through the air,
passing so close over his head that he felt the wind caused by
it stir his hair. Instantly Ysabel lunged forward, thrusting
out the deadly knife with savage force.

Too late Bitter Root saw his danger. Blind fury had driven
him beyond all caution, spurred him into stupid, uncaring
recklessness. Against a fighting man of Sam Ysabel's caliber,
such a mistake was fatal. Although he tried desperately to
halt or twist aside and avoid the knife thrust his impetus
carried him inexorably onward to doom. Even as his free
hand struck down in a vain attempt to block Ysabel's attack,
he felt a numbing, burning sensation in his stomach.
Shocked pain wiped the fury from his face as he realized
that he had been unable to either stop his advance or block
the knife's thrust.

Ysabel felt the clipped point of the bowie dig into flesh,
then the razor-sharp blade continued to sink deeper. Such
was the design of the James Black bowie, the finest fighting
knife ever made, that it sank hilt-deep into Bitter Root's
belly almost of its own volition. Instinctively Ysabel ripped
the knife sideways. He felt the rush of hot stomach gas on
his hand, then the sticky dampness of flowing blood as he
tore the man's belly wide open. A strangled cry broke from
Bitter Root's lips. Jackknifing over as the knife sliced clear
of his flesh, the stricken man staggered forward a couple of
steps. His hands clawed ineffectively at the hideous mortal
wound and he crumpled to the ground.

Before the dying man landed at his side, Ysabel came
erect and brought his blood-dripping knife into the on-guard

position. The precaution proved to be unnecessary. While a
rumble of talk welled up among the onlookers, it held no
censure for Ysabel's actions. Incidents such as just witnessed
were no novelty among the *Pehnane* and other bands of the
Comanche Nation. Born and raised to be fighting men, the
braves possessed proud, touchy natures which refused to
turn the other cheek when insulted or abused. Formal duels
never happened. Any affront received prompt settlement of
a definite nature.

Nor did the fact that Sam Ysabel had a white skin affect
the issue. When he took initiation into the Dog Soldier
lodge, he became classed as a full-blooded *Pehnane* and received all a Comanche's privileges.

If it came to a point, Bitter Root could not claim *Pehnane*
blood either, being an Apache captured as a child, adopted
as a son by his captor and made a full member of the band
by virtue of his skill as a fighting man.

Maybe there would have been trouble if Bitter Root stood
high in his war lodge's favor. His general attitude, plus a
lack of those virtues by which a brave became liked, prevented him from gaining the admiration of the other members of the Owl lodge. So none of them felt any responsibil-
ity in the matter, or wished to avenge his death.

Wiping clean his knife blade, Ysabel scanned the crowd
until locating the senior Owl lodge member present.

"My apologies for spoiling your game," the big white man
said formally.

"You have good cause?" inquired the Owl lodge leader.

"Good enough," Long Walker put in and indicated the
body. "Has that one a brother?"

"No. He has four wives. None of them will mourn him
greatly—"

"Except the one called Fire Dancer," put in another
member of the Owl lodge. "She bore him a son only a few
days ago."

"I will send them blankets and four horses," Ysabel
promised.

The words brought a mumble of approval from the listen-ing crowd. As the insulted party, Ysabel did not need to raise a finger to help the dead man's dependents. Doing so increased his standing in the band and made less likely any attempts at reprisals by hotheaded, name-seeking Owl lodge *tuivitsi.*

Leaving Long Walker to explain the cause of the visit to the assembled gamblers, Ysabel and War Club collected their horses and rode back to the Dog Soldiers' camp area. There the Indian explained to his wives what would be needed and Many Brothers rose immediately to obey.

On his return to the birth tepee, Ysabel found all ready for his wife's funeral. After he entered the tepee and paid his final respects, the waiting women completed their work. Folding the blanket around the body which rested upon it, they bound it firmly in place. Ysabel brought up Raven Head's favorite horse and left it before the tepee, withdraw-ing to the fire and standing with his head bowed in grief. Carefully the women carried out the body and lifted it on to the waiting horse. One of the sisters mounted and sat on each side of the body, holding it in position, then the party rode slowly from the camp. Three miles from the village, to the west of the lodge in which she died, Raven Head was laid to rest in a deep crevice on top of a high hill. Her sisters placed her facing to the west in a sitting posture and the weeping mourners covered her in a mound of rocks, bushes and earth.

Standing alone after the departure of the rest of the party, Sam Ysabel said a silent, half-forgotten prayer. Then he took out his bowie knife and slit the throat of his wife's horse, tumbling its body into the crevice so that its spirit might serve her in death.

"Adiós, querida," he said gently. "I'll care for the boy."

With that, he turned and walked to his patiently waiting grulla. Swinging into the saddle, Ysabel rode slowly away from his wife's grave and down toward the *Pehnane* village where his son drank thirstily from the breast of Many Brothers.

Whatever fate the future held for Loncey Dalton Ysabel, at least he would not now starve to death.

3
Early Days

While the death of a woman called for extensive mourning on the part of her relatives, including the destruction of her personal belongings and the tepee in which she died, much more was expected from the bereaved of a name warrior. In the case of a highly respected and well-loved husband, the wives would gash open their faces, breasts and limbs, keeping the wounds open, raw and irritated for months. Sometimes the wives would cut off all their hair, an ear or a finger to show their sense of loss. Often they remained at the grave, wailing and mourning, refusing all food, until forcibly removed by relatives concerned for their safety and health.

The wives of Bitter Root, with one exception, showed only such grief as needed by convention. A harsh husband with mean, cruel ways, he held the affection of only one of his four wives. That one, like Bitter Root, had been a captive. Born in a small Mexican village, the woman fell victim to a Comanche raiding party while still a young child.

Brought north to the *Pehnane* country, she lived as a slave to her captor's family and grew into a slim, fiery, beautiful girl with an amazing skill at dancing. She also possessed another talent, as shown when taken as third wife by Bitter Root. In a short time she ousted the first wife and assumed the position of *pairaivo*. Only Fire Dancer never felt the surly wrath of Bitter Root and she lived very well, especially when compared with the other wives.

Seated in her tepee on the night of Bitter Root's death, Fire Dancer realized that life would not be so easy in the future. The other wives were not going to forget her abuses and all had families ready to take their part. Already the other three spoke loudly in her presence about the manner in which their dead husband's wealth would be divided. Unless otherwise stated by its owner, a dead man's property—such items as were not by tradition destroyed—was shared equally between his wives. Fire Dancer had hoped to gain far more than a mere quarter, but knew that the opportunity to do so had gone. From being the *pairaivo* of a wealthy warrior, one single afternoon reduced her to the position of a comparatively poor widow dependent on charity to feed her and the tiny baby in the cradleboard upon her knee.

Brooding on the wickedness of life, Fire Dancer looked down at the baby, a boy destined by a medicine man's prediction to become a fine brave and great war leader. No matter how her son grew up, Fire Dancer swore that he would have one purpose in mind; to take revenge on everybody connected with his father's death. If possible, she aimed to help him in the task.

One thing she wanted to do was get away from the *Pehnane* village. All too well she could imagine her fate at the hands of the other wives and neighboring women she had given cause to hate her. Until the boy grew older, it would be best if they sought fresh pastures. Recalling that she had heard a small party intended to go on a visit to the *Kweharehnuh,* Antelope, band which made its home in the Tule and Palo Duro country, Fire Dancer decided to ask

permission to accompany them. Only when the party returned to the *Pehnane* village, she did not intend to be with
it.

Hanging the cradleboard on her shoulder, she left the tepee and went in search of the party's leader. On hearing the
woman's story, he gave permission for her to travel with
them. Next day, after the division of Bitter Root's property,
Fire Dancer rode away from the *Pehnane* camp. It would be
many years before she returned, but time would do nothing
to change her feelings or lessen her desire for revenge.

Not knowing that he had made an enemy by killing Bitter
Root, Sam Ysabel also made plans. Much as he hated the
thought, he knew he must leave the village and return to his
duty. A combined army of Texans and regular United States
soldiers fought to establish once and for all who would own
the Lone Star State. Men like Ysabel, who knew the country
and how to live in it as well as the best ways to fight Mexicans, were badly needed, so he knew he must return.

"I'll be riding after the name-giving ceremony," he told
Long Walker as they sat smoking their stone pipes by the
chief's fire.

"It is good," Long Walker answered quietly. "War Club's
women will care for the child until you return and I will
watch over him."

"I knew that without telling," Ysabel assured the other.

That evening a good-sized crowd gathered before Long
Walker's tepees. Bringing the infant from War Club's dwellings, Many Brothers prepared to deliver him to the chief
Pehnane medicine man, who would perform the name-giving ceremony. Although a public affair, the name giving had
to be carried out inside a tepee. After the main guests had
been settled inside, *Tawyawp,* senior medicine man, made
his dignified entrance. First he lit his pipe from the tepee fire
and directed puffs of smoke to the earth, sky and four major
points of the compass. With this done, he raised a prayer to
Ka-Dih, the Great Spirit, asking that the baby's future be
long and successful. Then, laying aside his sacred medicine

pipe, he accepted the naked, squirming child from Long Walker's *pairaivo*.

Raising the baby into the air, *Tawyawp* intoned the words, "His name will be Loncey Dalton Ysabel."

Four times he repeated the words, fumbling a little over the strange non-Comanche names, raising the baby a little higher into the air on each repetition. At the end of it, Loncey received his name in as correct and formal a manner as if some circuit-riding white preacher performed the ceremony in a church, anointed his head in water and inscribed the child's full title in the family Bible.

Despite the family being in mourning for Raven Head, grandson's baptism had to be celebrated in a fitting manner. Ysabel and Long Walker did well in the supplying of food and presents for the guests. Singing, dancing, the telling of great deeds performed, lasted all night and the name-giving ceremony was conducted in a manner guaranteed to ensure Loncey a life of length and success.

Despite his rousing and hectic send-off, Loncey Dalton Ysabel did little beyond eating and sleeping during the first nine months of his life. Once the name-giving ceremony ended, he was carried back to his foster mother's tepee and returned to the cradleboard. Having her own son to care for, Many Brothers only fed Loncey. The rest of the time, the *pairaivo* saw to his needs. Each night the *pairaivo* removed him from the board, washed, greased and powdered him tenderly and carefully. At night Loncey slept comfortably in a bed built inside a stiff tube of rawhide, the latter to prevent him from being crushed should the *pairaivo*—no featherweight—roll on him during her sleep.

At no time did Loncey receive different treatment from Many Brothers' son, Loud Voice. He might have been the women's own flesh and blood, the loving care and attention they lavished upon him. During his sixth month, a marauding bunch of Kaddo bucks raided the village. When the howling braves tore between the tepees, the *pairaivo* caught up Loncey and dashed for safety. She carried the boy with her stocky body between him and the attackers, determined to shield him from flying arrows.

When he reached the ripe age of nine months, Loncey found himself freed for the first time from the cradleboard and allowed to learn the delights of creeping about the tepee. Watched over by the women and older daughters, he progressed from traveling on hands and knees to tottering upon two bare feet. He put on weight to such an extent that the *pairaivo* could no longer carry him on her back. As he outgrew the cradleboard, so his method of transport changed during the time when the village made one of its periodic moves. Instead of hanging suspended from the *pairaivo*'s saddle, he graduated to sharing a place on a travois pulled by a gentle, steady pony.

Being fighters and hunters who grew no crops, the *Pehnane* needed to change locations at regular intervals. In a very short time, the boy grew used to traveling and as he increased in age the more fun it became.

During the first four years of his life, Loncey ranged the *Pehnane* hunting grounds from the Pecos River to the Cross Timbers Belt and along the headwaters of the central Texas rivers. He saw a vast amount of country while suspended from a saddle, or perched alongside Loud Voice upon a travois. His foster parents treated him as their own and his maternal grandparents gave him attention. With the Mexican War over, Sam Ysabel returned and continued his life of hunting, selling meat, hides, furs and wild horses to the ever-growing ranches and settlements. Loncey soon grew to respect the big white man and considered himself very fortunate in having so many people deeply concerned with his welfare.

One morning at about the time of his fourth birthday, Loncey found his grandfather waiting for him as he left the tepee. Something in the chief's attitude gave the boy, young though he was, a warning that Long Walker did not just happen to be on hand at that particular time.

"Come, *tawk*," said Long Walker, using the common term
by which grandfather and grandson addressed each other.

No Comanche boy was ever led by the hand and Loncey
strutted along proudly at his grandfather's side, wondering
what might be in the air. Certainly it would not be any kind
of punishment. For one thing he had done nothing to merit
it; and even if he misbehaved, it would not be his grandfather or parents who handled his correction. That task fell
upon his oldest foster sister. Even she did not employ physical punishment, but directed the misbehaving child with
persuasion or threats. The parents and grandparents merely
presented the child with object lessons in good behavior.

Side by side, Loncey and Long Walker passed from the
boundary of the village and went to a small valley a short
distance away. Realization began to creep up on the boy as
he saw a small pony standing picketed in the valley.

"It is time you learned to ride like a *Pehnane, tawk*,"
Long Walker informed him, confirming his thoughts.

"Will I be a braveheart warrior then, *tawk*?" piped the
boy eagerly.

"In time," smiled the chief. "You do not want me to
fasten you on the god-dog's back with a rope, do you?"

Already Loncey possessed a certain pride. Puffing out his
tiny chest, he shook his head. "I do not, *tawk*."

Taking hold of the boy under his arms, Long Walker
swung him up and perched him on the pony's back. Despite
his casual refusal to be secured in position, Loncey could not
hold down a nervous gulp. While the pony stood only twelve
hands, its forty-eight-inch height seemed to tower far above
the ground. Determined not to allow any sign of fear to
show, Loncey sat rigid and straight. Glancing at his grandson, Long Walker started the pony moving slowly forward.
Used from birth to the motion of a traveling horse, Loncey
found it vastly different when seated astride. Grabbing hold
of the mane in both hands, he clung on until the knuckles
showed white, while his legs clamped on to the pony's ribs

and gripped tightly. Slowly his nervousness left him and a feeling of exhilaration replaced it.

"Faster!" he screeched excitedly.

Then he felt himself falling. Overconfidence caused him to relax his hold and the slight increase in the pony's pace altered its gait enough to throw him off balance. Generations of horse savvy brought about an instinctive reaction. Instead of trying to stiffen himself and control the fall, a sure way to get hurt, Loncey's body remained relaxed. Given time to think, he might have acted otherwise. The fall, coming so unexpectedly, did not allow time for thought. Landing on the ankle-deep buffalo grass, Loncey bounced once and lay winded, fighting to hold down the tears which pain induced. Slowly he raised his eyes and looked up into his grandfather's face. He read no derision or condemnation; nor did he see any of the concern the chief felt.

"Are you hurt, *tawk*?" asked Long Walker.

"N—No."

A potential braveheart warrior did not admit that a mere fall from a pony jolted his rump severely and painfully.

"Then get up."

Slowly Loncey rose. Not without some misgivings did he feel himself swung up onto the pony's back once more. However, he set his face into a grim, determined mask and took a firm hold.

"I am ready," he said, trying to sound a whole heap bolder than he felt.

"This time watch what you are doing," warned Long Walker.

Before the boy had time to think of the fall and become afraid, Long Walker started the pony moving. Being forced to concentrate on staying astride prevented Loncey from worrying about losing his seat and in a short time the old feeling of pleasure returned.

After a short time the boy caught the knack of staying astride. With his background and breeding, riding came almost easier than walking. He quickly learned how to main-

tain his balance and by the time noon came could stay with
the horse at a walk and up to a steady trot. In the afternoon
he progressed to sitting the pony while it circled Long
Walker at the end of a long rawhide rope.

"You have done well, *tawk,*" said Long Walker as the boy
slipped from the pony's back at his command.

"Can I ride some more, *tawk*?" Loncey piped eagerly,
ignoring the ache in his legs and body.

"Not this day," smiled the chief. "Your pony is tired, and
so am I."

So, if he cared to admit, was Loncey; more tired than he
could ever remember being. For all that, the boy felt happy.
Small and young though he might be, Loncey realized that
he had taken an important part and major step in his life.

With the possible exception of the buffalo, nothing was
more important to the Comanche than the horse. It offered
him more than a means of transport and mobility. Alive, the
horse carried the Comanche or hauled his property from
place to place; allowed him to run down the buffalo and
assisted in hunting other animals; bore him to war, enabling
him to strike fast and over vast distances, or make good his
retreat should that become necessary; was a source of wealth
and prestige, a valuable gift and an acceptable item of barter.
Nor did the horse's usefulness end with its death. Its flesh
could—and often did—provide a meal when the hunting
failed or time prohibited the seeking of game. Shelter, robes,
saddles and rawhide thongs were made from its hide, the
mane and tail being converted into ropes and bridles. Without the horse, a Comanche became static and useless. Seated
astride the "god-dog," he was master of all he surveyed.

Unlike some of the horse-Indian tribes, the Comanche
held the horse in high esteem and rarely mistreated it. Each
man possessed at least one favorite mount which he tended,
petted and trained, keeping it picketed close to his tepee at
night while the rest of his string—which might run into
dozens or scores of animals—grazed among the band's remuda upon the open range beyond the village. To kill, or

attempt to harm, a favorite horse classed as murder. In the event of a legal dispute involving the payment of damages, whatever else might be claimed, the prosecution party almost always asked for the defendant's favorite horse to be included.

So learning to ride ranked among the Comanche boy's prime achievements in life and probably the most vital part of his existence.

From that day Loncey would spend much of his waking hours with horses, especially while learning to ride. Guided by Long Walker, Ysabel and War Club—both of whom he called *'ap,* father—War Club's brothers and oldest son, he spent hours on the gentle pony. From the men he learned how to care for his pony; when he must not allow it to eat and drink; by what means greater speed could be raised and maintained; the ways to keep the pony silent when it wished to whinny a greeting to others of its own kind and move it noiselessly from place to place. Trained by masters of all matters equestrian, he gained a knowledge of horse handling second to none. Galloping, swimming, jumping the pony, staying on its back under all conditions and over any kind of country, soon held no terrors for him. He learned to fall off without injury and to quit the pony's back voluntarily, landing safely no matter what its speed. Before he reached his fifth birthday, he felt as much at home on a horse as afoot.

By the time Loncey reached six years of age, he left behind the gentle pony and rode bareback on a young colt. With his long hair, black and shiny as the wing of a raven, and his body clad only in a breechclout, tanned Indian dark by exposure to the elements, he might have been a pure Comanche. Only his face set him apart from the other *Pehnane* boys. Instead of the brown-eyed, high-cheekboned, broad face of the Comanche, Loncey looked European. There was an air of innocence about his handsome features that the wild red-hazel eyes belied. In build, he stood taller and more slender than his companions. Those were only externals. He spoke Comanche naturally and English halt-

ingly only when in his father's presence. Underneath his
baby-faced innocent appearance beat the heart of a true
Pehnane.

In addition to learning to ride, Loncey received other lessons. Before he celebrated his sixth birthday, he knew which
roots, berries and plants could be eaten and where to find
them. Lighting a fire with either the fire bow or using a flint
and steel formed an important lesson. He learned the value
of patience and silence; a valuable lesson which would save
his life many times in the future.

Not all the schooling was on practical matters. From
Long Walker, Loncey learned the tribal history. At some
time in the past, the *Pehnane* moved away from other bands
of the Comanche Nation. Despite their name, which meant
the Wasps, Quick Stingers, or Raiders, the *Pehnane* lived in
comparative peace with the Texans and Mexicans whose
towns and settlements bordered the eastern fringe of their
territory. One reason for their being left in peace probably
stemmed from their very able means of defending themselves.

During their separation from the Antelope, Yap, Liver-
Eaters, Wanderers and other smaller bands of the Comanche
Nation, the *Pehnane* never forgot to which tribe they be-
longed. Long Walker smoked the peace pipe with Plenty
Kills, war chief of the Kiowa—from which tribe the
Pehnane adopted the war lodge idea—but remained, in the
best Comanche tradition, the enemy of all other Indians.
Even the Kiowa retained the old-style title for the Comanche, saying *"Tshaoh,"* the Enemy People, despite their truce
with the *Pehnane.* The Comanche referred to themselves, no
matter to which band they belonged, as the *Nemenuh,* the
People, and spoke the word with a pride of race and achievement.

Although Ysabel spent a fair amount of time away from
the camp, Loncey did not feel neglected. All his companions' fathers went off on raiding, hunting or war trips of
varying duration, so he considered it only natural that

Ysabel did so too. One way and another, life was too full and interesting for the boy ever to feel lonely.

He became a skilled hand with a lariat early, learning how to send its running noose flickering out to drop on a horse's neck. While on the march, he helped herd the spare horses as became a useful young member of the band.

Early in his sixth year, Loncey went into another stage of his education. Long Walker presented the boy with his first bow and a few blunt-headed arrows. Once equipped, the boy received every encouragement to practice. In addition he also learned how to make arrows and build a bow, for there might come a time when he needed that knowledge.

Unaware of the political and social changes taking place in eastern Texas, almost without knowledge of other white men, Loncey spent his early childhood contentedly. While keeping the peace with the white man, Long Walker did not encourage too much contact and apart from hunters, or an occasional visit of state by a company of Texas Rangers, had little to do with them.

In the future Loncey would become involved in the affairs of the Lone Star State, taking an important part in some of them, but during the first six years of his life, he knew nothing of them. His time was fully occupied in learning those things he must know to become a braveheart warrior of the Comanche Nation.

4

Loncey Meets *Piamempits*

Shortly before his seventh birthday, Loncey performed an act which became the first step in making his name among his people. The *Pehnane* had been moving toward their pre-winter buffalo hunting ground for almost two weeks, traveling through most of the daylight hours and throwing up a hasty temporary camp at sundown. At last they had reached the desired area and the various lodge chiefs told their people to halt and settle down.

Having reached the end of their journey, the younger boys found themselves free from the task of horse herding. At such a time, boys and girls of from six to about ten gathered in bands to play. Loncey ran with one of the groups consisting of children from Dog Soldier lodge families. Already his group had built up a reputation for high-spirited behavior and the knowing among the lodge members nodded in satisfaction, saying that Loncey, his foster brother and another of the group, Comes For Food, showed the signs of making true bravehearts if their present actions be any sign.

On settling down for any length of time, the mixed groups sought out a deep hole in a nearby stream and made it their gathering point. Thinking back to the previous year's visit to the area, Loncey recalled the ideal spot for their play camp. One small snag arose as he suggested the location; it lay beyond the Dog Soldier tepee area. Unless the group moved fast, a bunch from the Fox lodge might reach the place first.

"They have a shorter ride to it," Loud Voice warned.

"Not if we go through the camp," replied Loncey and ran to where his pony stood waiting.

Eagerly the rest of the boys collected their mounts, going astride the bare backs like squirrels climbing a pine tree. Kicking his heels against the pony's ribs, Loncey started it moving. Always willing to join in any kind of fun, the remainder of the boys followed Loncey's lead. Ten colts and ponies raced away from the horse herd, to tear at speed through a camp busily engaged in setting up homes.

Riders racing through the village had never been so rare a sight as to excite comment. The women grew accustomed to erecting tepees in the face of such distractions. Normally the riders showed sufficient consideration to keep their running horses away from the working women. However, on this occasion Loud Voice sat afork a slightly larger, more spirited colt than usual, and lacked the strength to control it properly. So while his companions steered their mounts clear of trouble, he found his heading straight into it.

Following his usual practice, old Sleeps Long And Deep, skilled bow maker of the village, stood close by so as to supervise the erection of his main tepee. While his wives secretly objected to what they regarded as an unwarrantable intrusion into their domain, they could do nothing to change the old man's ways.

Already much of the work had been completed. After fastening the four fourteen-foot-long cedar poles at the upper end, the women stood them erect, spreading the lower

ends outward evenly as the start of a circle. Against this
foundation a further eighteen poles, their butts sunk about
two feet deep into the ground for added strength and security, rose up to be tied to the main poles. Using the pyramid
of poles as a skeleton, the women hung the carefully cut and
fitted buffalo hides into place to form the walls of the dwelling.

All this had been completed and the women worked on
the final outside task, that of fastening the buffalo-hide covering at the top. A task calling for some skill and knowledge,
fastening the top and arranging the tepee's smoke hole fell
upon the oldest, most experienced wife. Sleeps Long And
Deep's *pairaivo,* showing remarkable agility for an elderly
woman, stood on the shoulders of his other two wives, from
which vantage point she had already pinned the covering's
edges together with wooden skewers about the size of a
white man's pencil and fastened the top into position. When
Loud Voice made his hurried appearance, the old woman
leaned forward to fix the smoke hole. By folding the upper
skins back a short distance, giving the appearance of a jacket's lapels, then fastening the turned-back sections to poles
outside the tepee, the hole made could be shielded from the
wind and create a draft that sucked the smoke from inside.
Leaning forward precariously, the *pairaivo* could not have
picked a more inconvenient position had she tried.

Being astride a fast-running horse, even one almost out of
control, held no terrors for a Comanche boy. As he tore
along, Loud Voice whooped in delight and showed how he
gained his name by the volume of noise he could turn loose.
He shot at an angle between the tepees of Sleeps Long And
Deep and the *tsukup*'s next-door neighbor, coming into the
tepee builders' view unexpectedly. Seeing the charging pony
headed straight at her, the youngest wife not unnaturally
decided to avoid being run down. Unfortunately she forgot
that the *pairaivo* perched insecurely with a foot on her
shoulder. With a shriek, the woman flung herself backward
and the *pairaivo* found herself deprived of one support. Let-

ting out a howl of mingled surprise, fright and anger, the
pairaivo lost her balance. Her other foot slipped from the
second wife's shoulder and she fell forward. While sturdily
constructed, the tepee lacked its final supports. The
pairaivo's weight, being at the upper part, caused the tepee
to collapse.

Never noted for a mild, even temper when things went
wrong, Sleeps Long And Deep did not view the incident
calmly. Showing some speed on his feet, he nimbly avoided
the falling tepee and leg-waving, curse-screaming *pairaivo*
and so came to no actual harm. However, he knew that he
would not be fed until after the erection of the tepee and,
being a man who enjoyed food, did not care for the idea.
Letting out a screech of rage, he shook his fist after the
whooping, delighted, departing youngsters who regarded the
affair as a glorious joke.

"May *Piamempits* take you!" he howled.

None of the youngsters took any notice of the words, being more concerned with reaching the desired play area before any other band arrived. Watching the departing children, Sleeps Long And Deep snorted angrily. Despite the
fact that they tended to act soberly and show a serious outlook when in the presence of strange white men, the Comanche people possessed a well-developed sense of humor and
enjoyed their fun the more if it be boisterous and visual. So
the mishap at Sleeps Long And Deep's tepee brought about
much mirth among the onlookers.

Followed by laughter, which did nothing to lessen his
wrath, Sleeps Long And Deep stalked angrily off in search
of War Club; Loncey and Loud Voice being the acknowl-
edged leaders of that particular bunch of youngsters. Although War Club and Ysabel—the latter just returned from
a most profitable trading trip to the white settlements—
managed to put on a straight, unsmiling face by the time the
tsukup reached them, they declined to take any action
against the boys. True it did not become very young Comanches to treat a respected *tsukup* and craftsman in such a

manner, but one had to excuse their wildness as part of growing up to make useful warriors.

Nor did Sleeps Long And Deep receive any more comfort on carrying his grievance to other members of the family circle. Loud Voice's older brother and paternal uncles—the latter classing as his father by Comanche tradition—only laughed. While on a less formal basis than War Club's brothers, the *ara** took a more definite line in the matter and stated that no punishment would come to the boys. As a sop to Sleeps Long And Deep's wounded pride, however, the *ara* presented him with a week's supply of wapiti meat. That had always been the Comanche way, the *ara* and his nephew being on an easygoing, friendly footing. Any boy could treat his *ara*'s property as his own and rely on the other's support and protection should he get into trouble.

In the face of such determined opposition, Sleeps Long And Deep obtained no satisfaction for his injured dignity. The offer of a week's supply of meat, while tempting and generous, did not lessen his determination to carry the matter further. By the time he returned to his tepee area, he had decided to take firm action himself lest the boys grow up with no respect for old age, wisdom and dignity. With that thought in mind, he told his wives that he would need certain items which had proved most useful on other occasions when discipline had been required for the children.

Unaware of their impending lesson, the children reached their selected site and gained possession by right of prior occupancy. Swiftly they set about building the miniature village which would form their home during the daylight hours as long as they stayed in the area.

While regarding their activities in the light of play, the children spent much of their time performing tasks which fitted them for their future life. The girls erected small windbreaks, for shelter, such being woman's work, and prepared the fires ready for the return of the boys from foraging mis-

* *Ara*: Maternal uncles.

sions. Already Loncey and his companions knew how to locate birds' nests and collect the eggs. They knew which kinds of plants might be eaten safely, the kind of berries they must avoid and could differentiate between edible and poisonous mushrooms.

Nor did they stop at vegetable matter for their food, but hunted with their bows and blunt-headed arrows. Showing that skilled coordination between hand and eye which would one day make him famous as a rifle-shot, Loncey excelled in the matter of driving an arrow into and killing the large grasshoppers which leapt and fluttered about. Once killed, the grasshopper could be roasted over a fire and made a much-prized delicacy. Rabbits, chipmunks, squirrels, prairie dogs, small birds or anything the boys' arrows could bring down gave bulk to the meals. The boys hunted with grim determination, never relying on the fact that they could obtain a meal in the village if they failed to lessen their attempts. They were encouraged to be self-reliant, taught to fend for themselves and praised when they succeeded. Although the game might sometimes fail, the *Pehnane* rarely faced prolonged periods of starvation such as the Shoshone and other more northern tribes met. In winter food might be short, but that had to be borne. Even so the foraging boys often had a full belly gained by their own efforts when their parents tightened belts and made medicine to guide them to deer, elk or buffalo.

Not all the time in the play area was spent in hunting or housekeeping practice. In the late afternoon, after a meal of baked grasshopper, gopher, piñon nuts, pigweed, the inner bark of a birch tree and bulbous roots of the sego lily, the children decided to play "Grizzly Bear."

Going out onto a large, sandy bank of the river, the children built a mound of sand. Loncey and Loud Voice upended the youngest member of their band and dragged him around the mound by his heels until they smoothed down the surface. With everything ready Loncey stepped onto the smoothed-down area to be the "grizzly bear." Outside the

circle Loud Voice formed the others into single file, each
child holding the preceding one's waist.

"Now!" commanded Loud Voice and advanced, leading
the line toward the level area.

Crouching slightly, Loncey watched the line approach
him. As the "grizzly bear" he had to protect the mound of
"sugar" and also try to catch the "mother," Loud Voice, or
one of the youngsters.

For a time Loud Voice managed to keep his "family" safe.
Swinging the line back and forward, he steered them clear of
Loncey's grabbing hands. However, the white boy's slim
build gave him added speed that enabled him to cover the
"sugar" effectively and prevented the others from stealing
any of it. Then one of the girls in the line made the mistake
of coming too close. Out shot Loncey's right arm and the
girl screeched as his fingers closed on her shoulder. Instantly
the line broke up and the children scattered, leaving the girl
to be hauled into the circle to be "eaten," which meant nothing more serious than a tickling administered by the "grizzly
bear."

On making the first capture, Loncey changed the course
of the game. Instead of a single line coming, now he had to
protect the "sugar" from the individual rushes. Darting in,
the children either grabbed off a handful of sand or were
captured and "eaten." Such games developed hard, tireless
muscles, especially when acting as the "grizzly bear," and
Loncey showed no signs of tiring even after defending the
"sugar" continuously for over an hour. All the girls fell victim early in the game, but the boys proved more elusive.
Darting around, leaping over the mound, flashing from side
to side, Loncey captured boy after boy, "eating" them and
sending them to watch from the sidelines. Of course he
could not protect the entire area at once and the mound
diminished gradually as the number of boys decreased.

Comes For Food evaded Loncey until the last. With the
complete circle to move in and only one assailant to watch,
Loncey could protect the "sugar" easily. Making a feint at

going left, Comes For Food lunged suddenly to the right. Shrieks of delight rose from the spectators as he reached the edge of the circle. Then Loncey, pretending to be fooled by the feint, turned and dived forward to lock his arms about the other's waist. Together they crashed to the sand and sat up grinning at each other.

"What now?" asked Loud Voice, coming forward.

For a moment none of the others replied, but all glanced up toward the sky. Already the sun had sunk down in the west and long shadows spread over the land. With the excitement of the game over, the youngsters became aware of the passing of time. Night would soon be on them and all cast darting looks in the direction of the main village's glowing fires. Each of the youngsters remembered stories, told around the winter fires of their tepees, about *Piamempits,* the Big Cannibal Owl. As the sun sank in the west, *Piamempits* left his home cave in the south slopes of the Wichita Mountains and flew in search of his favorite food, young children who had behaved badly during the day.

"Let's go back to the village," suggested one of the girls, throwing scared glances at the gloomy darkness of the riverside woods. "Perhaps *Piamempits* will be so hungry that he cannot tell the difference between good and bad children."

While the words caused most of the children to think about returning home, they tended to have the opposite effect upon Loncey and Loud Voice. Soon the two boys would reach the age when they put aside childish things, ceased playing with little girls and joined the all-male band of adolescent youths in learning to be warriors. So the two boys did not wish to rush back to the village just because the sun happened to be going down.

"Shall we have another game of 'Grizzly Bear'?" asked Loncey, trying to sound bold and casual.

"Why not ask a *tsukup* to come and play 'Do You?' with us?" Loud Voice answered, attempting to appear unconcerned by the possible danger of *Piamempits.*

Loncey nodded his agreement. Before they could play at

"Do You?" an old man had to volunteer his services in the game. Few *tsukup* ever refused such a request, but finding one meant returning to camp. Once there the group could break up and return to its various homes, giving its leaders an excuse for not returning to the play area without any hint of being afraid of *Piamempits*.

"We can ask old Tamina," Loncey said. "He will always find time to play."

"Let's go then," replied Loud Voice. "I know where to find h—"

At that moment they all heard the eerie, spine-chilling sound of an owl hooting among the trees—only sounding far louder than the cry made by any normal bird. Being shrewd practical students of nature, all the party realized that no ordinary owl produced such a volume of noise. Instinctively the youngsters bunched closer together and with their leaders before them. Again the owl hooted, closer than before. One of the girls let out a scream of terror and pointed off toward the nearby trees. Following the direction she indicated, the remainder of the party saw a sight which chilled them to the marrow.

Coming out of the darkness was a vague, unreal white shape which looked neither animal nor human. Long white wings fluttered, spreading out menacingly, as the thing advanced on the children and again came the hooting of the owl—from the approaching thing.

"Piamempits!" screamed a girl.

Which exactly matched the thoughts reached by every member of the band and fired them all with the desire to escape.

Another hoot rang out from the creature and it darted forward like an ordinary owl swooping upon a fear-frozen mouse. Instantly the party scattered, screaming and shrieking in terror as they darted toward the safety of the village. Last to surrender the field were Loncey, Loud Voice and Comes For Food. Showing commendable courage, they allowed their younger companions to flee first, then whirled and ran themselves. In going Loud Voice caught his foot on the top of the depleted mound of "sugar" sand, tripped and went crashing to the ground. He rolled over and let out a howl of terror as the shape bore down on him.

Hearing and recognizing his foster brother's voice, Loncey skidded to a halt and twisted around. While as scared as any of the others, Loncey saw his "brother" in trouble and showed something of the kind of man he would grow up to be. Flinging himself forward with a juvenile attempt at a war yell that was three parts fear, Loncey hurtled over his fallen "brother" and crashed headfirst into the fluttering white shape. The force of his arrival brought a startled, very human-sounding grunt of pain from the thing, causing it to reel backward and sit down hard. Unable to stop himself, Loncey landed on top of the shape and bore it backward until it lay flat on the ground. Sheer instinct for self-preservation caused the terrified youngster to launch wild blows at the shape, while his lungs churned out screeches loud enough to waken the dead and drowned certain sounds made by *"Piamempits."*

Loud Voice sat up, amazed to find himself still alive instead of being carried away by *Piamempits.* Then he saw Loncey and guessed what must have happened. A leg, looking surprisingly human, showed from the white form of *Piamempits* and waved wildly before the boy's face. Grabbing hold of it, he sank his sharp teeth into its calf and hung on like a bulldog laying hold of a beef-critter's nose.

Attracted by the screams of the children, men in the village raced for and bounded astride their horses after snatching up the nearest weapons. They expected an attack by some enemy as they charged toward the direction of the sounds and rode prepared to make a fight. Passing the fleeing children on his way out of the camp, Sam Ysabel noticed Loncey was missing and cold anxiety bit at him. He gripped the butt of the Walker Colt holstered at his side and swore vengeance should a hair of the boy's head be harmed by the attackers. Gun in hand—he had inspected the revolver de-

signed to Captain Walker's recommendations, decided it was
worth owning and so bought one—he reached the sandbank
first of the rescue party. Sliding the grulla stallion to a halt,
he stared at the sight before him. The Colt's barrel sagged
groundward and a bellow of laughter broke from him.

Flat on his back, raising a tolerable fuss considering his
disadvantages, with Loncey seated upon his chest throwing
punches at him and Loud Voice gnawing at his leg, Sleeps
Long And Deep emitted bellows of mingled rage and pain.
Other men drew their horses up and joined in the laughter
as their eyes took in the scene. Every one of them could
guess what had happened.

One of the methods used by the Comanche to throw a
scare into misbehaving children was for an old man or
woman to drape him or herself under a white sheet—looted
from some Mexican or white owner—and come down on the
mischievous ones as Sleeps Long And Deep attempted to do.
Normally such a shock would have worked, in fact almost
did on this occasion. Only the *tsukup* failed to take into
account Loud Voice's accident and the sturdy spirit and
loyalty of Loncey Dalton Ysabel.

"It seems we have a warrior for a son, Ysabel," grinned
War Club as the two boys came to their feet.

"Looks that way," agreed Ysabel.

"This was a brave deed for one so young," Long Walker
put in and the men about him rumbled their agreement. "He
must be rewarded."

"Would it be in order for us to give one so young a Give-
Away Dance, *naravuh*?" Ysabel inquired.

"I think it would," the chief answered and again the assembled braves gave their approval.

When a young Comanche performed some feat of courage, his family held a Give-Away Dance in his honor.
Loncey became the youngest member of the *Nemenuh* to
receive the honor.

Four days after the affair, the tribal drummers gathered
by Long Walker's fire, facing east in the center of a large

crowd. A grave-faced, specially coached slip of a boy danced the victory steps and several *tuivitsi* honored him by joining in. Loncey's father, foster parents, grandfather and a number of other people pitched presents at the youngster's feet as he danced. Several blankets, a knife, sticks which represented horses, landed in the circle. Even Sleeps Long And Deep made a present, a stronger bow than Loncey's present weapon and a half-dozen arrows.

Anybody who wished among the spectators could grab up one of the presents and claim it. Of course no warrior would think of doing so, for that would imply he could not raid well enough to gather his own property. Women took the opportunity to obtain blankets and a couple of old men in need of horses took up a tossed-in stick. The deeds implied a tribute to the recipient of the dance, showing that those who helped themselves believed he could quite easily produce more property by his skill as a raider.

Following the Comanche tradition, Sam Ysabel gave away the entire profits of his last trading trip. He knew he could easily earn more and that by giving he ensured himself of help when he needed it.

As for Loncey, the *Pehnane* told each other of his exploit. By common consensus of public opinion, he would grow up to be a great warrior worthy of assuming Long Walker's war bonnet if he kept up such a high standard of courageous conduct.

5

A Reward for Diligence

After his sudden rise to fame, Loncey found the public's eye upon him more than ever. He was expected to set his companions a good example and generally did so. However, little changed beyond making sure that his band did not charge through the camp and create a disturbance. The acquisition of a more powerful bow allowed him to try his hand on larger game. Often he and his friends attempted to bring down the swift-flying bullbats in an evening time. While they occasionally managed to hit a bat, their light bows lacked the power to hurl an arrow hard enough to bring the animal down. Using his new bow, Loncey finally achieved his ambition. With a leather cuff around his left arm to protect it from bruising by the string—a necessity with the more powerful bow—he practiced shooting at stationary objects first, graduating to moving targets. Not for several tries did he bring off his desired coup on a bullbat, but when he did his whoop of triumph could be heard all around the camp.

Word drifted back to the *Pehnane,* carried by visiting braves, of Fire Dancer's activities among the *Kweharehnuh.* Soon after her arrival, she attended a dance and her skilled grace attracted the attention of a wealthy warrior. A marriage had been arranged and, following the pattern established in the *Pehnane* village, she took over the position of *pairaivo.* Shortly after the warrior made a public announcement that Fire Dancer must receive the bulk of his property when he died, he met a sudden, mysterious end. A second husband followed and the pattern repeated itself. By all accounts the wealthy triple-widow had found yet a fourth man willing to succumb to her charms and fast rose to the position of *pairaivo.*

What none of the news carriers told was how the woman raised her son in his father's light—she bore no more children—and taught him to hate those she blamed for Bitter Root's death. Only Fire Dancer knew of her hate, but that made it none the less deadly.

One day soon after Loncey received his Give-Away Dance, a party of Texas Rangers rode into the camp accompanied by other men who wore strange blue clothing which looked all alike. It seemed that Texas, including all of Comancheria, had at last been persuaded to turn from its status as a republic and become a member of the United States of America. A condition laid down in the agreement was that the United States supplied troops for keeping the peace and policing the land and Texas disbanded the Rangers. At that time the Rangers consisted of unpaid volunteers, so they raised few objections to being able to return to their homes and interrupted lives. Before disbanding, one company of Rangers escorted a company of U.S. Dragoons on a tour to meet the various friendly Indian chiefs. Knowing the quality of the *Pehnane* fighting men, the Rangers wanted to make sure that the Dragoons knew enough to avoid ruining the friendly relationship existing between the two peoples.

Actually it would be some time before the change from republic to state of the union affected the *Pehnane*. They paid no taxes, made no trouble and asked only that they be left in peace. So far not sufficient settlers had reached Texas for there to be any need to encroach upon the Indian lands and, without pressure from potential voters, the government at state and national level saw no reason to go to the expense of antagonizing a people who wanted only to remain friendly.

Life went on as before for Loncey. By the time he reached his eleventh birthday, he started the final training which would end when he rode upon his first war trail as a braveheart warrior. When Sam Ysabel returned from his last trip, he brought back a Green River fighting knife and Long Walker set to work to make a sheath for it. Without being told Loncey guessed the knife would be his when the men felt he deserved it. That day would mean that they also considered him old enough to progress to his warrior training.

While waiting for the day, Loncey continued his normal existence. More and more his age group tended to mingle with the older boys and ignore the younger, mixed group of children. They played rougher games, relegating "Grizzly Bear" and "Do You?" to their past. Wrestling lessons and instruction in the art of knife fighting became their prime interest; with Loncey showing an affinity for the latter which made his teachers nod in grim approval. Of course the French Creole shared with the Comanche a love of cold steel for a fighting weapon. How Loncey, wielding a wooden knife, longed for the day when he wore the real thing at his side and could master throwing it; a most important part of handling a knife as a fighting weapon.

Increasing age brought advantages. When younger Loncey and the other children often found themselves commanded by older boys to assist in a game of *Nanip'ka,* "Guess over the Hill." In one version the youngsters had to hide under buffalo hide or blanket covers on one side of a hill and the boy who was "It" came around to try to guess the identity of the children under the hiding places.

In the second version, which Loncey preferred, the boys selected a hiding place among the natural cover and the "It" player had to locate them. Playing that version taught the youngsters the value of concealment and how to be patient, staying perfectly motionless for long periods despite all discomforts. The knowledge Loncey gained playing *Nanip'ka* would save his life on more than one occasion in the years to come.

When not commandeered by the older boys, Loncey's group played the game among themselves and he developed an ability second to none at locating the hidden players.

One day soon after his eleventh birthday Loncey stood on a slope as "It" in a game of *Nanip'ka*. So engrossed did he become that he failed to notice his grandfather close behind him and watching every move he made. Time after time Loncey pointed, called a name and location and brought one of his companions from the place in which he located the boy. At last only Loud Voice, no mean hand at *Nanip'ka* himself, avoided detection.

For almost fifteen minutes Loncey raked the ground before him with keen-eyed attention. He examined every bush, rock, tree and depression without result. Overhead a hawk made a leisurely circle in search of food. After glancing at the bird, Loncey brought his eyes hurriedly to earth. In a moment he found the cause of the slight movement which drew his attention from the hawk. Sliding through the grass, a king snake made its way toward a small clump of mesquite. It moved at speed, not caring for the open nature of the surrounding land. Instead of darting into the shade and security of the mesquite clump, the snake swung away and wriggled rapidly up the slope to disappear beneath a rock.

Loncey noted the snake's actions, also that the hawk did not drop down and take advantage of the easy prey. As neither creature behaved in a natural manner, he studied the mesquite once more. Previously he passed over the clump as being too small to hide anything larger than a jackrabbit.

"Loud Voice!" he called, taking a chance. "Behind that small clump of mesquite close to the two small rocks."

A laugh greeted his words and Loud Voice emerged from the hollow he dug behind the mesquite. Behind Loncey, Long Walker nodded approvingly. It had only been a few seconds earlier that he located the hidden youngster. Stepping forward the chief asked Loncey how he found Loud Voice's hiding place.

"You did well, *tawk*," Long Walker declared after hearing Loncey's explanation. "Come back to the village with me."

While walking back to the village, the chief repeated the story of how he made peace with Plenty Kills of the Kiowa.

"We each cut our wrist and mixed blood, *tawk*, swearing an oath to Ka-Dih that each and the family of each had the right to ask and receive of the other. Remember that well, Loncey."

"I will, *tawk*," promised the boy.

The day would come when Loncey visited the camp of Plenty Kills and made use of the blood oath.*

Back at Long Walker's tepee, the boy sat eating a hearty meal and listened to his grandfather's tales of great and daring deeds. When the meal ended Long Walker rose and entered his main tepee. On his return, he held out the sheathed Green River knife to Loncey.

"Tomorrow we hunt, *tawk*," the chief said.

Letting out a whoop of delight, Loncey bounced to his feet. Then he caught hold of himself. A man of eleven summers did not act in such a manner, especially as he was being taken on his first real hunt in the morning.

Unlike when going to war, hunting did not call for a man's best clothing. Long Walker left his war bonnet in the tepee and dressed in a plain buckskin shirt and fringeless leggings. A tomahawk rode in his belt slings, balanced by a

* Told in *Guns in the Night*.

James Black bowie knife, while a quiver of arrows hung over his shoulder. While he owned a Mississippi rifle, the chief did not use it for hunting. He could shoot with accuracy, but found a bow more suited to his needs.

Made of Osage orange, the *bois d'arc* of early French explorers, the bow in Long Walker's left hand was the type found to be best suited to a Comanche's needs. Only three feet in length, it could be handled easily from the back of a fast-running horse and yet still packed sufficient power to drive a thirty-inch arrow feather-deep into the body of a bull buffalo. It had been made by Sleeps Long And Deep, costing Long Walker twenty horses, and the chief regarded the price as reasonable.

Being newly arrived in the area, the village had not yet done much hunting. So Long Walker expected he would be able to show the boy some success on his first trip. He did not allow the youngster to take a bow, but Loncey felt satisfied.

Game roamed in abundance in the area. Not only did the buffalo herds graze on its rich grass, but wapiti and Texas whitetail deer could be found in fair numbers. It was the latter that Long Walker sought.

Never one to waste time, Long Walker took advantage of every opportunity to teach Loncey something of use. They did not rush, but looked into every bit of sign they came across and the chief explained its meaning. At last, after covering some four miles from the camp, Long Walker saw what he wanted. Slipping from his saddle, he motioned the boy down from the bare back of his spirited colt.

"Deer fed here this morning, *tawk*," the chief said and told Loncey how to read from the torn edges of the cropped grass the length of time elapsed since the upper section had been ripped away by the animal's teeth. "Nothing frightened it, so we may find it among those trees up there."

"We will find it," Loncey stated.

"Perhaps," smiled Long Walker. "But we must make sure

we see the deer before it sees us. That means walking slowly
and little, looking a lot."

Trembling with eagerness, Loncey watched his grandfather slide an arrow from the quiver and place it into position
on the bow. Then side by side they advanced along the
deer's tracks toward the trees. Already the boy knew the
Indian way of walking silently, by placing the ball of the
foot to the ground first and only lowering his heel when sure
that nothing which might roll or snap lay underneath.

The boy had little to learn about the need for silent movement and his ability in that line had already brought him
one sizable meal. During a period of food shortage Loncey
ranged far from the village and came on a flock of wild
turkeys. Although the turkey had not yet developed that
wary alertness brought about by excessive hunting—and
which would one day make it highly prized as a sporting
game bird—one did not stalk and drive an arrow into a big
tom without silent movement and using cover. Loncey had
killed a tom turkey that day. All the basic rules of stalking
he had used on that occasion served him just as well now.

Without giving any sign or hint of doing it, Long Walker
studied the boy's behavior. Shortly after entering the trees a
satisfied smile came to the chief's face. He saw Loncey,
about to step on a dry stick, pause balanced effortlessly on
the other leg and move his raised foot beyond the danger
point. It seemed that the boy learned well and did not allow
excitement to fluster him.

Silently and slowly the man and boy advanced through
the woods. They kept the wind in their faces and made
many halts to scan the country before them. Long Walker
felt pleased that they did not come quickly upon their
quarry. A long difficult search would test the boy's patience
and teach him the persistence so often needed when hunting,
raiding or making war.

A brief flicker of movement attracted Loncey's attention
during one of the halts. His quick eyes focused on the place
but for a moment failed to detect anything. Then the thing

moved again and he made it out to be the ear of a big white-tail deer; a buck lying among a clump of blueberry bushes, its antlers merging into the background so thoroughly as to fool the casual eye. Only the movement of the ear gave the animal away.

Loncey glanced at his grandfather. To his surprise it seemed that the chief failed to locate the deer. Instinctively the boy prepared to draw Long Walker's attention to the animal, then realized that a word or sudden movement would startle it and drive it into flight.

Slowly, inch by inch, the boy raised his hand to touch Long Walker's sleeve and in the same cautious manner indicated the deer's position. At the same moment the buck rose, not frightened but sensing danger and looking for it.

Having already seen the buck, but waiting to study Loncey's reactions on locating it, Long Walker was ready. In a single fluid motion he raised the bow, drew back its string of plaited grizzly-bear sinews and sighted the arrow. Once sure of his aim, he released the string. Out flickered the arrow, made from a young shoot of the flowering dogwood tree, so highly prized for its straight growth and lack of knots, with triple turkey-feather flights. Being used for hunting, the razor-sharp steel arrow head bore no barb and was set on the same plane as the bow string so as to pass between an animal's ribs—the war arrow always carried a barbed head set at right angles to the string as it would be launched at a target which stood erect upon two feet.

Faster than the eye could follow, the arrow sped toward the buck. Up to twenty yards, Long Walker reckoned to hit an object the size of an apple four times out of five, and the buck stood broadside on within that distance. Even as the buck sensed its danger, the arrow sliced between its ribs and into its chest cavity. Unlike a bullet, which killed by shock and tissue damage, an arrow brought death by bleeding. So, although struck hard, the buck did not go down. On the impact it bounded high, landed on feet already running and crashed away through the bushes.

"We've lost it!" Loncey said, a touch bitterly.

"Perhaps, perhaps not," Long Walker replied. "Let us take a look."

Darting forward, the boy plunged into the bushes. His eyes scoured the ground so as not to overlook any sign that might help him find the wounded buck. Standing back, Long Walker looked on and followed only when Loncey found the marks left by the buck landing from its first leap then dashing away.

"Look!" the boy ejaculated, pointing to the ground. "Blood!"

"The wound is a bad one," Long Walker answered. "We should find the buck soon, so move carefully."

Later there would be time to go into details of what might be learned from a blood trail. A man who knew the signs could tell the nature of the wound by the color and amount of blood spilled and Loncey would have need of that knowledge.

Despite the serious nature of its wound, the buck ran for well over half a mile. In doing so it had left the wooded area and lay halfway up an open slope. Clearly it had just realized the coverless nature of the slope and started to turn back to the shelter of the trees when it went down, for it lay facing the woods.

On coming into sight of their quarry, Loncey let out a whoop of delight. Before his grandfather could speak, he whipped up the slope toward the buck. Knowing something his inexperienced grandson overlooked, Long Walker halted his hand as it reached for another arrow and he followed Loncey as fast as his legs would carry him.

When the boy came near it, the buck suddenly let out an enraged snort and lurched upward to launch a savage hook with its antlers at his body. At that moment the skill and agility developed in childhood games like "Grizzly Bear" came in mighty useful and saved him from being disemboweled. Skidding to a halt, he threw himself desperately aside, twisting his lean young frame with the speed of an otter-hunted eel. Even so, fast though he moved, the antlers brushed against his arm in passing. Off balance, Loncey went sprawling to the ground and he saw the buck start to swing in his direction.

Knowing there would be no time to draw and use another arrow, even if one could achieve the desired result quickly enough to be of use, Long Walker did not waste time trying. Instead he drew the tomahawk from his belt. Like the bowie knife, it had been a present from Ysabel and made in James Black's Arkansas forge. There was no better steel in the United States than that made by the Arkansas craftsman and it held an edge almost as sharp as a razor. Swinging the tomahawk around, Long Walker sent its blade crashing on to the back of the buck's neck. Steel bit home to sever the buck's spinal column. Instantly it went down, flopping to the ground as if boned, and almost landed on top of Loncey. Only by making a very hurried roll over did the boy avoid having the bloodspouting buck collapse on to him. A hoof, kicking spasmodically, struck him on the rump and brought a yelp of pain from his lips.

Slowly Loncey rose to his feet and turned a sheepish face to meet his grandfather's eyes. The boy knew that he had made a foolish, rash mistake even before Long Walker addressed him.

"Always look first before you go near any animal," the chief warned. "If it lies with its legs sprawled out, ears drooping, mouth open and face to the ground, it is either dead, or too badly hurt to be dangerous. If you had stopped and looked, you would have seen that the buck had its ears erect, legs doubled underneath it and head held up. That meant it was still sufficiently alive to be dangerous."

"I did not think, tawk," Loncey admitted.

"Then think next time. If that had been a grizzly bear or a cougar, you would be dead."

"Yes, tawk."

"Always treat any wounded animal as being dangerous. Don't go toward its head if you can come up on it from

behind. If it lies, like the buck, on a slope, go to it from
above so that it must charge uphill at you. And when you go
in close, be prepared to defend yourself, even if you feel sure
that the animal is dead."

Loncey nodded soberly, filing away the words for future
reference. Having made his point, Long Walker did not bela-
bor it. While Loncey might have made a foolish mistake, the
chief doubted if he would ever repeat it. So he praised the
boy's conduct throughout the majority of the hunt and nodded to where the Green River knife lay after being dropped
during his wild evasive action.

"Take up your knife, boy," Long Walker ordered. "I'll
show you how to butcher the buck now we've killed it."

"That is woman's work," Loncey objected, full of male
superiority now he had been on his first major hunt.

"And when there are no women with you?" smiled the
chief.

Taking the point, Loncey picked up his knife and waited
for instructions. He had watched the butchering of buffalo
after the big organized village hunts, but, as the work had
been done by the women, paid little attention to the details.
From the manner in which Long Walker handled the work,
Loncey decided skinning and butchering could be a task
worthy of a man learning.

There were even advantages to doing one's own butchering, Loncey admitted to himself. Having worked up a
healthy edge to his appetite, he found himself in a position
to do something about it. What was more, all the tasty titbits
went his way instead of having to be shared among several
more equally eager children.

Using his new knife, he deftly opened a vein and drank
the buck's warm blood as it flowed. Then he assisted his
grandfather to skin the animal, watching where to make the
incisions so as to remove the hide in one piece. While butchering, he ate well, sampling the raw liver soaked in the juices
from the gall bladder, raw kidney and its tallow and part of
the paunch. Later he and his grandfather sat down to a

favorite delicacy of their people, raw brains mixed with the marrow from leg bones using a section cut from the buck's rib cage to act as a dish.

By the time the butchering ended, Loncey felt he could not eat another mouthful. Leaving the buck's heart in the denuded skeleton to propitiate the Deer Spirit, Long Walker and Loncey loaded hide, meat and antlers onto the horses which the boy had collected. Pleasantly gorged and very happy, Loncey mounted his colt and rode at his grandfather's side in the direction of the camp.

6

Black Bear Hunt, Comanche Style

Once introduced to the art of hunting, Loncey spent much
time at it. Accompanied by his grandfather, Ysabel, or on
his own, he ranged the country around the village and
learned many lessons. After a couple of trips, Long Walker
allowed the boy to take along his bow and arrows. Not the
first, nor the second time did Loncey succeed in bringing
down the animal he hunted. A whitetail deer took much
more killing than a cottontail or jackrabbit and lived in
country which made hunting the more difficult to accomplish.

Soon after the first hunt, the village separated into smaller
groups. At that time of the year, the game tended to scatter
over a large area and the buffalo, mainstay of the *Pehnane*
existence, had gone north to its hot-weather grazing lands.
At such a time the full village could not find sufficient game
in one area and so broke up into various
war lodges or lesser numbers to range over their territory.

Before separating, *Tawyawp*, Raccoon Talker and the other
tribal elders made medicine to decide where the people
should gather again for the autumn buffalo hunting. On the
result of their estimations—be it by divine inspiration or just
plain guesswork backed by knowledge of the bison's habits
—depended the success or failure of the village's hunting
and the winter food supply for the people.

In many ways Loncey regarded the separation period as
the best part of the year. True, much of the social whirl,
dances, feasting, visiting other lodges, was to some extent
curtailed, but there were other advantages. With only the
Dog Soldier lodge families present, Long Walker need spend
less time in his capacity of chief and could give more of his
attention to his grandson's education.

The search for food took the Dog Soldiers across their
territory in the direction of the Waco Indian country, but
that did not unduly worry any of the braves. Like all other
Indians, with the exception of the Kiowa, the Wacos were
enemies and could be raided, supplying loot and coups to
the braveheart *Pehnane*. Of course some of the old men
pointed out that the Waco might regard the under-strength
village in the same light, but no warrior paid any attention
to such talk. *Tsukup* always took a gloomy, dull outlook,
having forgotten the joys of the war trail or put aside their
love of fighting.

While looking forward to a brush with enemies, Loncey
concentrated on his lessons in the martial arts. He spent
much time mastering the secret of throwing his Green River
knife, showing typical Comanche and French Creole affinity
with it as a tool and weapon. In addition, he now owned an
even stronger bow, one approaching full power, and must
improve his aim with it if he hoped to make use of its potential.

To help improve their skill with the bow and arrow, the
boys were encouraged to test each other in various contests.
Loud Voice and Comes For Food's education kept pace with
Loncey's and the trio frequently competed against each

other. Even though hot rivals at such times, nothing endangered their friendship.

Of the three, Loud Voice excelled when indulging in the speed test. In that, each contestant stood on a line and shot an arrow as high as he could into the air. Then he tried to discharge as many more arrows as possible before the first landed back on the ground. Loud Voice developed great speed and always managed to get off at least two more arrows than either of his friends.

When playing at *We'kere,* shooting at the mark, Comes For Food mostly won. To play *We'kere,* one of the boys fired an arrow so that it struck into the ground some distance away, the contest being to see who could shoot nearest to it. On one occasion Comes For Food actually split Loud Voice's shaft with his arrow at thirty-five yards.

Loncey came into his own when playing the most exacting game of all. To play *Aritisi,* the wheel game, called for quick reflexes and a keen eye. The wheel, a mere four or five inches in diameter, was rolled before the shooter at a distance of ten yards. Made of a willow rim coated in rawhide, the wheel had a one-inch hole at its center and the contestant scored points by hitting the rawhide, or sending the arrow through the central hole.

Playing the wheel game gave Loncey instruction in the matter of rapid aiming and allowing for alteration in position when shooting at a moving object. Even before going on his first hunt, he had learned how to aim ahead and continue swinging even as he loosed the arrow. Once he took to hunting, that knowledge became very useful.

Having already taken a whitetail doe while out with his grandfather, Loncey looked forward to making his first lone-handed kill. With that thought in mind, he left the village early one morning and rode in search of what he might find.

Not for three hours did he find any sign of game worthy of a braveheart hunter's bow. Once he came within easy arrow-shot of a jackrabbit, but allowed it to bound away unharmed. The gobbling of a tom turkey calling its flock reached his ears but he ignored it. Only in time of severe shortage did the Comanche eat bird meat and Loncey was not hungry enough to repeat his early exploit in turkey hunting.

Ranging through the open woodland which ought to have produced something that a young man might hunt, Loncey came to the banks of a small stream. Dropping from his dun's bare back, he allowed the colt to drink. While bending forward to slake his own thirst, Loncey saw something which made him forget it. Quickly wading across the stream, he looked down at what appeared to be the marks of a deer's hooves, yet were larger than any deer he had ever seen. Not even the big buck brought into the village triumphantly by Comes For Food the previous week approached the size of those hoofprints.

"Which means a wapiti made the sign," Loncey mused, breathing harder.

A wapiti. Loncey's heart beat faster at the thought. What a coup the killing of a full-grown elk would be. In size, strength and endurance the wapiti rated high in the Comanche's estimation. Eating its meat was believed to give the consumer some of the animal's vitality and power. Small wonder that Loncey hoped to hunt and bring down such a prize.

Quickly he hobbled his pony, leaving it by the water and with good grazing. Then, selecting an arrow with care, he crossed the stream and took up the trail. It said much for the boy's training that he managed to follow the tracks, for once they left the sand of the stream bank they did not show plainly.

After drinking at the stream, the wapiti returned to the trees but did not halt and rest as a whitetail deer would have. Instead the elk continued to move and Loncey followed on its tracks for a quarter of a mile without any sight of the animal's tawny hide. At last he realized that he would be unlikely to catch up to the elk while afoot. Returning the arrow to his quiver, he began to retrace his steps. After

collecting his horse, he could return and take up the trail
once more.

A scuffling sound brought Loncey spinning around and
sent his right hand to the waiting arrows in the quiver. He
stopped the move as a pair of bear cubs rollicked through
some bushes not far from where he stood. For a moment the
boy hesitated, undecided as to what action he ought to take.
The meat of a fat black bear tasted good, but a cub made a
poor substitute for the mighty elk Loncey hoped to kill. Nor
would any great skill be needed to make the kill. With the
characteristic inquisitiveness and lack of fear of all their
kind, the two cubs lumbered unconcernedly toward the boy.

Before he reached a decision, the matter left his hands in
no uncertain manner. Preceded by an explosive, rage-filled
snarl, the cubs' mother charged into view. Having already
caught the hated scent of man, she wasted no time and
charged straight at the boy. At that moment Loncey's bow
felt mighty inadequate and the sow bear looked a whole
heap bigger than her two hundred pounds weight. Turning,
Loncey fled for his life and headed to where a cottonwood
offered what he hoped would be a sanctuary from the fury-
bristling sow. While running Loncey discarded his bow, un-
slung and tossed aside his quiver of arrows. That left him
unencumbered and he went up that tree's trunk like a squir-
rel hunting its den hole. To his horror he found that one of
the cubs, startled by its mother's rage-bellow, had also fled
and climbed the tree. It perched on the most available
branch, backing away from the boy and squalling in a manner guaranteed to keep its mother's already riled-up temper
at full boiling point.

Climbing the tree no longer seemed like such a good idea
and became less so by the second as the sow began to ascend
the trunk. She came up looking all teeth, claws and showing
a desire to tear a *Pehnane* boy to doll-rags.

Drawing his knife, Loncey hung over the branch and
slashed down at the sow. Although he misjudged his aim,
the tip of the blade nicked the sow's nose and pain caused

her to slide back to the ground. Twice more she began to climb but each time the slashing knife drove her back. On the third occasion, the sow lashed out viciously and by the worst kind of luck struck the knife, snapping its blade against the tree trunk before dashing it from the boy's hand. The force of the blow unbalanced the sow, causing her to lose her grip on the tree and fall. Landing on her back, she rolled over and rose in a dazed manner.

For a moment Loncey thought he had won. Then the cub on the branch gave out another squalling cry which made her spin around and make for the trunk again. Suddenly Loncey realized that the sow would never leave without her cub. Backing hurriedly along the branch, he twisted around, grabbed the cub, pulled it free and dropped it straight onto the sow's head. Sow and cub went sliding to the ground in a heap. On rising, the sow let out a snorting command which sent the cub racing off followed by its earthbound brother. Ignoring the boy on the branch, the sow followed her offspring, bursting through the bushes and keeping going at a fair speed.

Loncey waited for some time before climbing down from the branch. Sorrowfully he took up the broken pieces of his much-prized knife and felt closer to tears than ever in his life as he looked at the wreckage. Fortunately his bow and arrows had suffered no damage, as he found on gathering them up. Sadly he turned and walked back along his tracks to his patiently waiting horse. He knew that he would have to explain the damage to his knife and wondered what his grandfather would say.

On his return to the village, shortly after dark, Loncey entered Long Walker's tepee. The chief studied his grandson and knew something troubled the boy. Laying his bow and quiver upon his bed, Loncey walked to the cooking pot and helped himself to the food.

"You found nothing, *tawk*?" asked Long Walker after the boy finished eating.

"No," Loncey replied and drew his broken knife.

"What happened?"

"A bear did it."

With his head hanging, Loncey told the full story of his adventure. Long Walker listened, his grave face showing no hint of his feelings. At the end, Loncey sat and waited to be condemned for failing to make a better showing in the affair.

"You acted wisely, *tawk*," Long Walker finally said. "The bear is a good mother and will fight to death for her young." Then, seeing that the boy still felt a sense of failure, he went on, "Tomorrow you and I will hunt for the wapiti. Two men are needed to handle so big a kill and we'll need a pack-horse, too."

Even as he spoke Long Walker wondered if it would be advisable for him to take an extended hunt at that time. Two warriors had already gathered and gone on raiding expeditions, while several more men rode on other business, leaving only a handful of fighting men to guard the village and protect its property. Given a resolute leader, the remaining men ought to be able to handle things, despite their nearness to the Waco country. However, as supreme war chief, any defense necessary fell on Long Walker's head and he must organize the braves. There had been no sign of the Waco and Long Walker did have a duty to Ysabel too. He must see that the boy received correct education and every encouragement to become a good warrior. A successful hunt would reestablish the boy's weakened confidence. So Long Walker decided to take a chance on the camp's safety.

Next morning the man and boy rode away from the camp, Loncey leading a packhorse and with one of Long Walker's knives sheathed at his side. Although they made an extensive search, they found no sign of elk. At noon they halted and made a meal of some jerked meat the chief brought along. Soon after resuming their hunt, Long Walker brought his horse to a halt.

"You see?" he asked.

"Death birds gathering," Loncey answered, recognizing

the distant whirling specks in the sky as circling turkey vultures.

"We will see what they are after," the chief stated.

Never one to waste an opportunity, Long Walker insisted that Loncey showed how well he had learned his lessons in the art of cautious travel. They did not know what they might find under the circling vultures, so acted as if they stalked a dangerous enemy. Keeping to cover, avoiding being skylined or otherwise exposed to hostile eyes, they rode toward the birds. Long Walker noticed with satisfaction that Loncey remembered and put into use the lessons given to him in that vitally important part of a warrior's trade.

After covering about two miles, doing so in a manner which would have taxed a watcher's ability to locate them, Loncey and the chief came in sight of the cause of the gathering of vultures. On their arrival, the birds rose into the air again.

"A doe," Loncey said and his nostrils quivered in distaste as the wind carried a stench of death to him. "Something has been eating it."

"Whatever it was, it isn't close by now," Long Walker answered. "The death bird is a coward and does not come down if the wolf, cougar or bear is near to protect the kill. We will leave the horses here and take a closer look."

With arrows strung ready for use, Long Walker and Loncey walked slowly and alertly toward the dead doe. Taking precautions against an unexpected return of the doe's killer, one of them watched while the other examined the injuries.

"A cougar made the kill and was dragging the doe to cover when a bear came and drove it away," Long Walker announced after his examination. "Since then the bear has eaten regularly."

Just a hint of worry crossed Loncey's face as he searched the surrounding country for some sign of the bear. Until the previous day he would have been eager to tackle the bear, wanting to progress to bigger game than the whitetail deer.

After his unsettling experience with the sow and cubs, he did not feel so sure of himself and had no wish to be disgraced in his grandfather's eyes by showing fear during a hunting encounter.

"Is it long gone?" he asked.

"Not long, or far. No bear would travel far with a full stomach. There are its tracks. It is not a grizzly."

Just a hint of relief showed in Long Walker's voice. He saw a chance to restore Loncey's confidence, but did not want to tangle the boy in the hazards of hunting a grizzly bear. Watching the boy, Long Walker read indecision on the handsome young face. However, Loncey sucked in a deep breath, gathered himself up and forced himself to say the words his grandfather hoped to hear.

"Shall I follow the tracks, *tawk*?"

"Bear meat is good," the chief replied. "Let us see if we can get some."

Following their established procedure, Loncey did the tracking while Long Walker followed close behind ready to assist should the boy run into difficulties. After leaving the doe, the bear ambled slowly down to a nearby stream, drank and then walked off at a tangent to the water. Loncey followed the tracks with no great difficulty, although not looking forward to the forthcoming encounter. Passing through some cranberry bushes, the boy saw a large hollow cottonwood tree which had been uprooted in some past storm and lay on the ground. The bear's tracks led into the yawning mouth of the tree.

A touch on the shoulder brought Loncey instantly to a halt. Obediently the boy sank down on his haunches and looked at his grandfather.

"The bear has gone up into his den tree," Long Walker explained in a voice barely louder than a breath. "Now he sleeps far up inside it."

"How can we get him out?"

"I will show you."

Two kinds of bear inhabited the *Pehnane* country; the

Texas flatheaded grizzly and the New Mexico species of the black variety. If the bear in the tree had belonged to the former type, Long Walker would never have thought of hunting it. Although the Comanche occasionally did hunt the grizzly—its sinews and tendons being prized above all others to be made into bow strings—they did so with extreme caution. Only seasoned braves, or *tuivitsi* seeking to make a name, went after *Ursus texensis texensis,* not a lone man approaching *tsukup* while instructing a boy.

The black bear did not rate that kind of respect in the Comanche's book. Certainly the plan outlined by Long Walker would not have been suitable for use against grizzly; but had been found acceptable when dealing with *Euarctos americanus amblyceps.*

Swiftly and silently Loncey and Long Walker advanced toward the cottonwood so as to put the chief's plan into operation. Walking to the upper end, the boy halted and waited until his grandfather reached the open bottom. Laying aside his bow, Long Walker drew the tomahawk from his belt. He turned and nodded to the boy then swung back and crouched alongside the opening. Although not sure of what his grandfather hoped to achieve, Loncey tapped gently upon the trunk with his bow. At first nothing happened, but as the boy repeated the tapping he heard a faint scuffling from inside the tree. Catching the noise, faint though it might be, Long Walker tensed slightly and concentrated on the mouth of the hollow trunk.

A sharp pointed black head with fairly large, erect ears and a lighter colored muzzle emerged from the tree trunk. Attracted by Loncey's tapping, the bear came to the entrance of its den and peered out. Before the bear could emerge fully, or sense the danger and withdraw to the comparative safety of the hollow, Long Walker sprang forward. Up swung his right arm, the sun glinting on the axe blade. Around and down swung the tomahawk, driven with all the strength of the chief's stocky, powerful body. Razor-sharp steel bit into the bear's skull, slicing through the thin layer of skin and penetrating the bone with the force of the blow. Instantly the bear collapsed, crumpling to the ground and giving only a few ineffective slashes with its legs before dying.

Due to its habit of occasionally walking upon its hind legs, the black bear was regarded by the Comanche as being closer to the human beings than any other animal they knew. So the slaying of a bear called for special medicine treatment if the hunter wished to avoid bad luck in the future.

"I am sorry that I had to kill you, furry black brother," Long Walker intoned formally. "But my people have need of your skin to keep them warm in the winter and your meat and fat to feed them now." With the required prayer of apology ended, the chief raised his eyes from the bear's body and looked at Loncey. "Always remember to speak those words when you kill a black bear, *tawk*."

"Don't I say them when I kill a grizzly?" asked the boy.

"No apology is needed when you kill the Great One, *tawk*. The black bear is a coward who can easily be killed—although a mother, or one cornered or wounded can be dangerous. The Great One, the grizzly bear, is not a coward. No man who hunts him need feel sorry when the kill is made."

"Is that why you killed with the tomahawk?" Loncey inquired, running his hand through the bear's fur and thinking how it looked much less impressive and dangerous than the sow had on the previous day.

"To kill with the axe is easier than with an arrow. The long fur slows down the arrow and prevents it sinking deep enough to kill."

One look at Loncey's face told the chief that he had achieved his intention. Long Walker had taken his chance to build up the boy's shaken confidence. By taking advantage of the situation and the bear's natural curiosity, he lured it out to its death—and showed Loncey that such an animal need not be feared.

"This is a man-bear, not the mother," Loncey announced after completing his study of the animal.

"Once you frightened her away, she would keep traveling for many miles," replied Long Walker. "As I told you, the black bear is a coward. Remember that and also that even a coward will fight sometimes. Now fetch the horses and we will take the bear to the village."

7

Bad News Rides a Fast Horse

When sport hunting became fashionable and impressive trophies the object of the chase, few animals would equal the black bear as a subject of exaggeration. To hear the claims of trophy hunters, weights of five hundred pounds and over formed the usual heft of a black bear. In actual fact, one which went over three hundred pounds could be counted as exceptional. The bear killed by Long Walker did not even reach the two-hundred-pound mark, so he and Loncey found no difficulty in performing the skinning and butchering.

With the butchering completed, they loaded the meat and hide between the packhorse and their own mounts, swung up themselves and set off toward their distant village. Sensing the slight disappointment at the short duration of the hunt, Long Walker promised that Loncey could try his hand on any worthy animal seen during the journey home.

Although he kept his eyes open, Loncey failed to see ei-

ther deer or elk. Not that he really cared, having fed well
and seen his grandfather perform a great feat. After passing
through wooded country for some time, they approached an
area of rolling, open plains.

Halting his horse, Long Walker gave a sign which caused
Loncey to come to an immediate stop. Eagerly the boy
scanned the land ahead of them, hoping to see a herd of
buffalo. It would be at least three more years before he rode
in the hunting party among the men when they took out
after the bison herds, but, like every Comanche boy, he
hoped for a chance to bring one down before that day. He
saw none of the shaggy-humped creatures, only two fast-
moving dots in the distance. Rapidly the dots grew in size,
taking shape as a pair of horsemen. After a few more seconds both Loncey and Long Walker recognized the riders as
a couple of young Dog Soldiers who had left the camp earlier that week with a small raiding party.

"It is Broken Nose and Bent Dogwood," Loncey remarked. "But where are the other four who rode with
them?"

"We will soon know," Long Walker replied. "Stay here."

With that he rode from among the trees and into view of
the approaching pair. Instantly they started to rein in their
horses. Then, recognizing him, continued to push their
mounts in his direction at a better speed. Having attracted
the braves' attention, Long Walker withdrew into the trees
once more. So far he could see no cause for alarm, but a wise
man took no foolish chances in a world filled with numerous
enemies.

Galloping up on their leg-weary, sweat-lathered horses,
the braves continued to move until joining the chief in the
cover of the trees. Once hidden from hostile eyes, the newcomers wasted no time in idle chatter for they brought
grave, serious news.

At dawn that day, while searching for somebody who
would serve to supply them with loot and coups, the raiding
party came across a large camp of Waco Indians. Studying

the Wacos without allowing their presence to be detected, the *Pehnane* party recognized two significant facts. Firstly they could not hope to accomplish anything against so large a band. Second, and more important, they saw that the Waco braves took down and stowed the tepees, having no women along.

Young though he might be, Loncey did not need to have the significance of the second detail explained to him. When traveling for peaceful reasons, an Indian took his family along so that the women could perform the menial tasks of tepee-erection and cooking. If the braves had left their women behind, it meant that they rode to make war.

"They are following along the tracks our village made as we came down here," Broken Nose stated.

"How many?" asked Long Walker.

"Ten hands at least."

Even allowing for some exaggeration, the braves would not be too far out in their estimation of the enemy strength. Fifty men in the Waco party put the odds well in their favor. At the most, even counting youths not yet old enough to be classed as warriors, the *Pehnane* village could at that moment muster no more than thirty. While every Comanche was expected to be brave, nobody could call him foolhardy. That meant a head-on battle was out. Yet the property of the village must be defended and prevented from falling into enemy hands.

"We'll get back to the village and make ready," Long Walker announced.

Without any further discussion, the party started their horses moving. Loncey rode alongside his grandfather, having drunk in every word said, and wondered what plans might be running through the chief's head. Three times during his young life there had been attacks by other tribes upon the *Pehnane*. On those occasions Loncey had been too young to take any active part. He believed that he could now lend a hand should it be needed and hoped to be given his chance.

Long Walker had almost forgotten his grandson as he sank deeper into thought. No general in the U.S. Dragoons, trained in warfare at West Point, ever gave more complete attention to details while planning an attack or defense. Using the experience gained during a lifetime of making war, Long Walker looked at the problem from every side.

Flight could be discounted straight away. No village, hampered by women and baggage animals, could hope to outrun an all-male war party. Covering six miles to the villagers' four, the Wacos must eventually catch up when the hard-pushed workhorses gave out.

Separating into small groups and scattering did not offer any better a solution. Many families did not have a grown man present and would fall easy victims to the pursuing enemy. All the Wacos needed to do would be select sets of tracks and follow them until finding their makers. After that it would be all too easy.

With two prime tactics inoperative, Long Walker saw only one alternative. Selecting their ground and taking every possible advantage, they must fight the Wacos and inflict such losses that the enemy would decide to run for safety.

Long before reaching the village Long Walker formulated a plan which might, given *Ka-Dih*'s blessing, work. He sent a crier around the camp to gather all available men at his fire. On hearing the news, the men came quickly. When all had assembled, Long Walker explained the position.

"Bad news rides a fast horse," he said. "But I have a plan that might work."

After hearing their chief's suggestions, the assembled men sat silent and thought on his words. Using his knowledge of the enemy, local geographical conditions and the strength of his own force as his guide, Long Walker planned well and none of the others could offer any alternative arrangement. However, one of his braves injected a comment.

"Who will guard the horses, Long Walker?"

A rumble of agreement went up from the others. Following Long Walker's plan would put the men selected in a

position of some danger. Naturally the danger drew volunteers, as any hazardous mission always did among honor-
seeking Comanches.

"I will be one," said Broken Nose.

"And I," went on Bent Dogwood.

"The Waco will not attack if they see *tuivitsi* guarding the
horse herd," Sleeps Long And Deep pointed out. "That is
the work of boys, not bravehearts."

Already Long Walker had foreseen the snag and knew
how to answer it. Yet the decision did not come easily to
him. Slowly his eyes went past the seated warriors to where
the boys of the village hovered in the background. By listening to the councils of their elders, the boys gained wisdom
and also learned the kind of manners needed when they too
joined the seated circle. Standing taller and slimmer than
any of the others, even the fourteen-year olds, Loncey took
no locating. Long Walker needed a brief moment of heart-
searching before he pointed to his grandson.

"Loncey," he said. "Come here."

With his chest puffed out to almost three times its normal
size in pride at being called to the council fire, the boy advanced. Squatting on his heels before his grandfather, the
boy tried to assume a grave, unemotional facial aspect simi-
lar to the braves around him.

"You heard what is wanted?" asked Sleeps Long And
Deep, studying the boy with an almost paternal interest.

"I heard," agreed Loncey eagerly.

"And you think you can do it?"

"Yes."

"Who do you want to be with you, *tawk*?" Long Walker
put in.

The task to be assigned to Loncey required the services of
three boys. Beyond the council circle eager boyish faces
tried to catch Loncey's eye. Not that he needed to look or
think.

"Loud Voice and Comes For Food," the boy announced.

"Do you think they will be able to do what's needed?"

inquired one of the young braves, conscious that it was his first time at the council fire and wishing to have his presence noticed.

"I think they will," replied Long Walker. "And they are just the right age for their task. Besides, we need all the older boys to help us fight."

For a time the discussion went on and Long Walker laid his plans. Few people in the world equaled the Comanche for being ruggedly individualistic and independent; yet when they put themselves under the command of a war leader—be he a fully appointed warbonnet chief, or a brave declaring that he aimed to take the warpath and needed volunteer companions—they obeyed his orders without question. Shrewd fighting men all, they recognized a born leader and accepted Long Walker as the best man to guide them through the forthcoming battle.

Much praise went to the bringers of the news for the sensible manner in which their party conducted itself; the more so considering that all six were *tuivitsi* riding for the first time without an experienced warrior along.

On locating the Waco band and guessing its intentions, the leader of the party immediately dispatched his two best-mounted companions to warn the village. Next he sent the remainder of his party to surround the Wacos and, remaining undetected, keep watch on the enemy.

Toward evening two more of the scouting party returned, bringing further news of the enemy. Any lingering doubts as to the Wacos' intentions died as the scouts told how the enemy party rode fast and ignored a herd of buffalo which made its appearance. Only men bent on war would pass up such a chance to collect meat and hides.

"They have two scouts out ahead," one of the *tuivitsi* told Long Walker. "Do you want us to go back and kill them?"

"No."

"But they will come and see the horse herd," objected the second scout, knowing what would be the prime target of the enemy.

"Then they will see what we want them to see," Long Walker explained, "and take word of it to the chief. Loncey, you know what to do?"

"I know, *tawk,*" agreed the boy.

"Then go and do it."

Riding through the gathering darkness far ahead of their main party, the two Waco Indian scouts kept alert and held their weapons ready for use. Yet, despite the careful watch, neither saw a sign of the *Pehnane* braves who preceded them in the direction of the village.

Cautiously topping a rim, halting just below it with only enough of them as necessary for looking over raised above it, the Wacos saw a sight which gladdened their eyes. Down on the floor of the wide valley beyond the rim grazed the *Pehnane* horse herd. Over a hundred horses and a number of mules stood, lay or moved leisurely, watched over by a trio of young boys.

"Only the boys guarding them," said one scout, the younger of the pair. "Shall we go down and take them, the village is at least half a mile away?"

Being more experienced in the ways of the *Tshaoh,* the Enemy People, the elder scout shook his head. "No. Their braves would catch up with us before we could reach our party. Let's go back and tell the chief what we've seen."

Although he did not know it, the words saved his and his companion's lives. Concealed close by, holding back their natural inclination to strike down an enemy, four *Pehnane* braves lined their bows and had orders to kill should any attempt at taking the horses be made before the arrival of the main Waco party.

Backing off the rim, the scouts made a long circle around the horse herd and reconnoitered the village. Neither felt particularly surprised nor suspicious at seeing how few men the village held. The summer had always been a favorite time for raiding and hunting. Their own village was also denuded of braves at that very moment. After studying the camp, the Wacos turned their horses and headed back to their companions. While doing so, they passed over the tracks of the second pair of returning *Pehnane* scouts, but by that time night had come and the darkness prevented the Wacos from seeing something which might have given them a grim warning.

A grin of satisfaction came to the face of White Crow, war leader of the Waco party, as he listened to his scouts' report. Mutters of delight rose from the other braves on hearing of the discovery of part, at least, of the *Pehnane* horse herd.

Any war party that entered the Comanche country came with one main object in mind, horses. Any other loot, scalps and prisoners would be acceptable, but were only secondary to the horses. Every Texas, New Mexico and Arizona Indian tribe gave the Comanche credit for being the supreme horse-masters of the red nations. Among the Indians, the Comanche stood almost unique in their attitude to horse breeding. Not for them to raise stock indiscriminately, so as to have prestige by numbers regardless of how the animals looked or worked. Instead the Comanche tried to improve the strain and supply himself with horses ideally suited to his nomadic way of life. Only the Nez Percé of the far West ranked with the Comanche in the quality of stock owned.

Small wonder White Crow felt pleased to hear of a good-sized Comanche remuda grazing in his path and watched over by what sounded like two *Pehnane* boys and a young white prisoner.

"Tomorrow at dawn we strike," he announced.

"At the village?" inquired a brave.

"We will take the horses first and drive them down through the village to waken those *Tshaoh* dogs. When they come out of the tepees, we can make a killing."

"The boys must be silenced before they can ride and give warning," a wily old brave counselled.

"Three wolf scouts will see to that," answered White Crow. "Take the boys prisoner if you can. But kill rather than chance them escaping."

While the Wacos made plans and contemplated a successful attack which would bring them much loot and many coups, the *Pehnane* village also prepared for the morning. Before the start of a raiding expedition or vengeance trail, an all-night dance put the bravehearts into the right mood and ensured *Ka-Dih*'s support in the proposed venture. No such precaution need be taken when defending the village against an enemy attack. Of course, given time to do so, a Comanche always applied his war paint and donned his best clothing before a fight. No member of the People cared to go into battle—even in a defensive action—unless dressed in a manner suitable for his entry to the Land of Good Hunting should he be killed.

Knowing that the Waco did not fight at night, Long Walker also realized that they could move during it. So he took no chances and prepared against a surprise visit to the remuda. After the Waco scouts left, Loncey's party returned to the village and a guard of half the fighting force gathered about the herd. All the other available men, including *tsukup* and boys not yet old enough to take the war trail, formed a circle around the camp, remaining alert and unsleeping through the night. Toward dawn, there having been no sign of the Wacos, the men needed for Long Walker's plan gathered in the village and made their preparations.

After dressing in his best clothing and applying his war paint, each man looked to his weapons. There had been a brisk trade among the arrow makers and every bow-toting brave's quiver held a good supply of barbed war shafts ready for use. Men with rifles checked on their powder and bullet supply, although their chief's plan did not call for much shooting, and loaded with care. Each knife and tomahawk's blade was tested on the ball of the thumb and brought to its best possible edge. Those among the men whose shield bore medicine power, to give spiritual as well as physical protection, went through the established ritual to collect the shield. A medicine-protected shield could not be brought into a tepee lest a menstruating woman came near to it or a person with greasy hands touch it, both being certain to destroy its power. So the shield must be hidden well clear of the village and its owner always made a full circle around the tepees when going to collect it.

Much as they would have liked to do so, Loncey and his two companions were forbidden to put on war paint or good clothing. The success of Long Walker's plan depended on everything looking natural when the Wacos arrived; and young boys guarding the remuda did not perform their menial task dressed as warriors.

Following their orders, the three boys acted just as they might be expected to after an all-night session of guarding the remuda. They sat in a triangle, patient ponies close by, with blankets draped over their shoulders and, despite the excitement bubbling inside them, looking more than half asleep. Never had they been more awake than as the dawn began to lighten the sky upon that morning.

"They're coming," Loncey whispered. "I can see one behind you, Loud Voice."

"I'm not sorry they're here," Comes For Food put in, speaking no louder. "It's cold and I'm hungry."

"You always are," grinned Loud Voice. "There's one coming down behind you."

"I can see another behind that clump of mesquite," Comes For Food stated, ignoring the comment. "He's after your scalp, Loncey."

The long hours playing at *Nanip'ka* paid dividends as the eagle-eyed boys detected the cautious advance of the Waco scouts. Against grown men the Wacos would have been far more careful, but made the fatal mistake of underestimating Comanche training. Most likely they would have succeeded had the boys really been on guard all night and not expecting an attack.

"There's no sign of the rest of them," Loud Voice commented.

"They'll be around, waiting for the signal from the scouts," Loncey guessed.

Moving in on the three boys, the scouts saw there would be no chance of taking prisoners. Although the slope offered reasonable cover, some fifty yards separated it from where the boys sat. Long before the scouts could reach them, the trio would be alerted, afork their waiting ponies and fleeing to the camp to raise the alarm. That meant, as the leader of the scouts knew, they must use the second alternative.

Across the valley, the third scout caught his leader's signal, knelt up cautiously alongside a rock and lined his bow on Loncey's back. To be of any use, all three arrows had to strike at the same instant. Should one boy be hit too early, the other two might avoid their arrows and escape. So the brave drew back his bow, sighted the arrow at the boy some fifty yards away, and waited for the signal. A glance told him that his companions on the other slope were ready. Then the leader released his bowstring and the other two followed suit only an instant later. Three barbed war arrows winged their silent, deadly way through the air toward the sitting boys.

"Now!" yelled Loncey, having watched the men behind his companions, even as the first arrow started to leave its bow.

Instantly each boy threw himself sideways and down, rolling clear of his blanket. The move had not come a moment too soon and every arrow would have found its mark had the boys remained seated. After the arrows hissed overhead, the boys sprang up and ran for the horses. Making a flying mount, Loncey landed afork the dun colt and started it running. No less agile, the other two sprang onto their mounts and headed for the remuda. Letting out wild yells, the boys startled the resting, grazing horses into motion and sent them running along the bottom of the valley in the direction of the distant, out-of-sight village.

8

A Lesson in Indian Tactics

Seeing the speed with which the boys moved, the scouts' leader wasted no time in notching another arrow and attempting to bring one of the fleeing youngsters down. There would be no chance to silence or stop all three, but maybe the remuda could be taken provided his party moved immediately. Throwing back his head, the scout let out a ringing wolf-howl. Clearly the Wacos possessed considerable skill in the art of silent horse-movement, for as the howl sounded hooves drummed out and mounted men swarmed over the top of either side of the valley. None of the Wacos needed explanations; they saw the fleeing remuda and knew that the plan to silence the boys had failed. Wild with humiliation, the scouts darted forward to bound onto the horses brought by their friends and joined in the chase after the remuda.

With the luster of already having received the honor of a Give-Away Dance, Loncey brought up the rear of the remuda and allowed his friends to ride on the flanks. Doing so put the boy in the most dangerous position, but it fell on Comes For Food to land in trouble.

Up on the right flank of the racing horse herd, Comes For Food's colt selected that moment of all times to drop its foot into a gopher hole. The colt went down, screaming as its leg broke, and pitched its rider over its head. Trained almost from birth at riding, Comes For Food felt himself going and lit down with catlike agility on his feet. Catching his balance, he flung himself toward the passing horses in an attempt to mount one. Although his fingers brushed a racing pinto's mane, he failed to obtain a grip and the horse brushed him aside.

Loncey saw the mishap and knew what he must try to do. Without a moment's hesitation, or thought for his own safety, the boy swung his pony to the right and urged it on at a better speed in the direction of his friend. There could be no greater disgrace for a Comanche than to leave an unhorsed, wounded or dead companion to fall into enemy hands and Loncey refused to bring disgrace upon his family by doing so.

Often at play the boys practiced the move Loncey aimed to make. A yell alerted Comes For Food and informed him that help came. Twisting around while still running, he saw Loncey tearing in his direction. Both boys knew just how difficult the rescue would be. A brave, seated upon the firm base of a saddle, could scoop up an uninjured companion while going at full gallop with no difficulty. To attempt the same feat riding bareback took skill, courage—and not a little luck. Leaning over, with one hand firmly locked in the pony's mane and legs clinging to the barrel of its body, Loncey reached down toward his friend. He caught hold of Comes For Food's wrist and gave a heave which assisted the other's upward leap. Even as Loncey felt they would tumble together from the pony, Comes For Food hooked a leg over its back. Given that much purchase upon a horse, any Comanche boy could stay astride it. Locking his legs instinctively the moment they felt the horse between them, Comes

For Food clung on behind Loncey. Despite their youth and lack of a saddle, the two boys had performed a mighty smooth pickup and only lost a little time in making it.

Furious at the failure of their original plan, the Wacos urged on their horses with rage-filled cries. White Crow saw a chance to still make something out of the failure. Guessing that the boys ran the horses toward the village, he kept his men moving. A stampede through the village would effectively prevent any cohesive defense happening and offer a chance of coups and loot.

Seated astride a magnificent paint stallion, his warbonnet trailing in the wind, White Crow drew ahead of his companions. He knew he must set them an example and prove the strength of his medicine. Reaching over his shoulder, he slid an arrow from his quiver. If his men saw him make a kill it would give them heart and increase their desire to count coup on an enemy. With that in mind, he urged his paint after the double-loaded pony.

Even carrying only Loncey the little pony would have been hard put to outrun the stallion; and with the extra weight of Comes For Food on its back it stood no chance at all. With each raking stride, the huge paint closed the distance and White Crow sat gracefully erect as he drew back the bow. A thought struck the chief and caused him to refrain from releasing the arrow. If he rode closer, he could drive his shaft through the body of the *Pehnane* boy into the skinny frame of the white "captive" riding before him. To kill both boys with one arrow would be visual proof of the strength of White Crow's magic and a feat to boast about around the Victory Dance fire on his return to the Waco village.

Closer and closer drew the paint, with its rider determined to make good the double kill. Even as the chief prepared to release his arrow, something swished through the air toward him. Sudden, numbing, sickening pain knifed into the Waco as a *Pehnane* war arrow sliced between his ribs and sank to its turkey feather flight in his chest. White

Crow jerked backward under the impact. Although he released his hold on the bow's string, his left hand jerked in a convulsion of agony and the arrow flew wild.

Kneeling concealed among a clump of cranberry bushes, Long Walker had watched his grandson's actions with considerable pride, but did not allow it to blind him to the boy's danger. Carefully he notched an arrow and drew back his own bow, aiming at the Waco chief. Much as he wanted to, Long Walker knew he must not shoot too soon. Scattered in cover on either side of the valley, which narrowed at that point, every able-bodied man and youth of the village waited for his signal before cutting loose on the enemy. If he started them too early, they would not have the Wacos far enough into the kill area and the trap might fail. So Long Walker hung on to the very limit of safety. Knowing the power of a war bow, he felt sure that the Waco's arrow would be able to penetrate Comes For Food and seriously injure Loncey even if it failed to make a double kill. Only when certain that he dare wait no longer did Long Walker release his arrow, sending it with unerring accuracy into the warbonnet chief's chest and tumbling him from the racing paint.

As might be expected from such excellent fighting men, the Comanche party obeyed their orders. They remained concealed and offered no hint of their presence until Long Walker's arrow gave them the cue to make their move. Gunshots crackled in an irregular volley as the men owning firearms cut loose. Arrows swished a near-silent and deadly way through the air toward the onrushing enemy.

Swarming forward eagerly, every man trying to be the first to catch up on the fleeing remuda, the Wacos could not have been better positioned to receive a volley of bullets and arrows. Chaos reigned as the leading men or horses went down and the riders in the rear tried in vain to halt their mounts before piling onto their fallen companions. Such a transition from attackers to attacked was guaranteed to demoralize and disrupt any force. So it proved with the Wacos, for they received no respite in which they might have recovered from their surprise.

No Comanche could sit back and watch an enemy from a distance under such conditions. To kill with arrow or bullet took no special courage in the People's eyes; even a squaw could do it. When a Comanche fought, he expected to count coup by personal contact rather than from a distance with his bow or firearm. So after that devastating volley, it would have taken stronger discipline than any *Nemenuh* submitted to for the braves to hold back.

Laying aside bows or firearms, the men caught up their war shields, drew knife, war club or tomahawk and launched a charge down on the disrupted Wacos. Hurt almost to death, White Crow still managed to lever himself onto his knees and reached for the Mills percussion pistol in his belt. Down charged a young *Pehnane tuivitsi* called Rains Coming, like a cougar tackling the last deer on a mountain. Ignoring the menace of the .75 caliber pistol, Rains Coming closed with White Crow. Around whistled the *Pehnane* war club, smashing into White Crow's head and laying it open.

"A'he!" whooped Rains Coming as the Waco chief's body tumbled to the ground and he sprang on in search of more glory.

Although shattered by the bloody, unexpected repulse, the dismounted Wacos prepared to sell their lives dearly. Those still mounted turned and fled, but the dismounted braves, knowing they could expect no mercy, fought back.

As a reward for the risk they took while acting as decoys, Loncey and his two companions had been given permission to watch the fight. Once through the kill area of the ambush, the trio allowed the remuda to race on and be collected by waiting boys who would halt it before it reached the village. Riding to the top of the valley's left side, Loncey, Loud Voice and Comes For Food came to a halt and turned to watch a bloody hand-to-hand mêlée after the classic example of Indian tactics.

Being a name warrior of high standing, Long Walker had
no further need to add to his fame. Already his family had
achieved distinction that day, with Loncey's courageous rescue of Comes For Food, so the chief felt he could allow the
younger men to go in first and have a better chance of counting coup. Such an action was not regarded as cowardly
among the *Nehenuh* when a name warrior did it. In fact he
received credit for his magnanimous behavior in foregoing
the chance to count coup in favor of the *tuivitsi.*

Even more important to the Comanche than loot and far
over the taking of a scalp—"Anyone can scalp a dead man"
—was counting coup: laying a hand upon the enemy. Some
tribes allowed the practice of counting multiple coups on a
single enemy. The Cheyenne permitted the first three men to
lay hands upon the enemy to claim him. Among the Arap-
aho, four braves could each count coup on a single victim. A
common belief among the Comanche was that Osage, lowest
of the Plains Indian low, allowed anybody who wished to
claim it, whether present at the time or not. That did not
apply to the Comanche, born fighters with sufficient enemies
to make such aggrandizement unnecessary. The People permitted two braves to share a coup only when the first's blow
came from a distance by arrow or bullet. Even then the main
credit went to the man who made physical contact with the
stricken enemy.

Bounding forward on the heels of the younger men, Long
Walker saw a sprawled-out Waco suddenly rise to one knee
and raise a rifle. By feigning death, the Waco avoided the
attentions of the charging *Pehnane* braves and saw a chance
of making a memorable kill before death took him. What he
failed to take into consideration was the shield on Long
Walker's arm.

Much time, thought and effort went into the making of
that shield, turning it into a first-class specimen of a highly
useful piece of Comanche warrior's equipment. Pieces from
the shoulder hide of an old bull buffalo, rated the toughest
kind of leather, had been steamed over boiling water until

thickening and contracting to the desired degree. While still hot, a careful rubbing with a smooth rock removed all the wrinkles and painstaking work cleared away any vestige of flesh remaining after the skinning. Four layers of hide were stitched flesh side out around a wooden shaping hoop, packing the spaces between the layers with feathers, hair, or— when it became available from the white man—paper to act as a cushion against the blows which the shield would receive. After the resulting circle had been molded into the correct saucer shape, a buckskin cover was fitted over it and two loops of rawhide, carefully adjusted to hold the finished product in just the right position upon the left arm, securely fastened to the concave inner surface. When thoroughly dried and hardened, the shield received a test. Set up against a tree, it had to deflect an arrow and bullet fired at it from a range of not more than fifty yards. If it failed the test, it would be cast aside as useless. Passing the test, the shield went into its final stage of production. Around the cover, a ruffle of feathers hung suspended by rawhide and upon the convex outside were the insignia of the owner. Bear teeth showed the owner to be a mighty hunter; scalps proclaimed a warrior of note; a horse's tail that he was a raider of the first water. Long Walker could claim to be one of the few Comanches with the right to show all three insignia.

Such a shield possessed flintlike hardness on its exterior with the layers of packing to act as cushions against impact. When on the left arm and moved by the warrior, the ruffle of feathers waved and weaved in a manner which distracted an enemy's eye and spoiled his aim.

Swinging his shield effortlessly, Long Walker positioned it between him and the Waco. He anticipated the other's aim and, as the rifle cracked, turned the shield slightly. At such close range the bullet might have pierced the shield if striking it straight on. Due to Long Walker's skilled manipulation, the bullet struck on the shield's curve and glanced off again harmlessly. Before the Waco could start to reload,

Rains Coming arrived and used the war club once more with deadly effect.

For several minutes the fight raged. Screams of dying mingled with war yells, cries for help and the Comanche coup yell of *"A'he!"* Then it was over and the only Wacos in the valley lay dead. Not until the last enemy fell did any Comanche worry about taking scalps. Swiftly the knives did their work, with Long Walker urging his men on. He wanted to get them back to their bows and guns in case the Waco who fled should return.

"Broken Nose, Bent Dogwood!" he called. "Go after them and see what they do!"

Flushed with the heady success of victory, the two men named turned and went to collect their horses. As it happened, they might have saved themselves a ride. One such defeat, which cost them some eighteen dead—not counting those wounded who managed to stay mounted, or were scooped up by companions—proved sufficient to damp down any Waco desire for Comanche horses and loot. The *Pehnane* were known to live up to their name, the Quick Stingers, so every Waco rode at his fastest and with the fear of Comanche vengeance in his heart.

Long Walker had no intention of taking a revenge-seeking party out after the Wacos. Given more men at his disposal, he might have done so. With the village so shorthanded, he declined to take the risk.

After seeing to the wounded, Long Walker went to where the three boys sat on the ground. All rose as he came near, trying to hide their excitement and look like men used to performing brave deeds.

"You did well," the chief told them and they could have asked for no greater reward than the words, especially as he continued, "Ride into the village and tell of our victory."

On returning from a successful warpath, raid or battle, the warriors always sent word ahead so that a fitting welcome could be arranged. Normally the youngest *tuivitsi* carried the word, but Long Walker gave the honor to the three

boys whose courage made the victory possible. In view of
Loncey's actions, the chief planned another reward for the
boy.

Everybody in the village gathered to hear the news. Eagerly they began to prepare a welcome for the returning
warriors, to be followed by a Victory Dance that night. Even
the families of the three men lost in the fight joined in the
preparations. Each of the dead men had counted coup before being killed and the People considered it to be a great
honor for a brave to count coup and be killed in the same
fight.

While the people in the village made ready, each warrior
freshened his war paint, tidied his clothing and put a shine
to his horse's coat with a vigorous rubbing by handfuls of
grass. Having counted coup twice, including on the Waco
warbonnet chief, Rains Coming was granted the privilege of
fastening one of the scalps he took to the lower lip of his
horse. That showed he had distinguished himself and ex-
pressed contempt for the defeated enemy. When sure all was
ready in the village, the men mounted. Led by Long Walker,
as commanding chief, and Rains Coming, the men rode toward the tepees.

Taking up a long, slender scalp pole, Raccoon Talker led
the people out to greet the returning braves. As medicine
woman of the tribe it was her right to do so and also to lead
the victory songs which welcomed the men home. In passing
the woman, each warrior who could tied a scalp to her pole.
Followed by the women, children and such men who had
not been involved in the fight, the braves paraded into the
village. After passing through the length of the village, the
warriors separated. Each man rode to his tepee, dismounted
and handed over horse and weapons to wife, mother or sister. While the women tended to the horses, the men rested
so as to be in good condition for the activities of the Victory
Dance.

After dark, a huge fire threw its glow of light upon Raccoon Talker's scalp pole as it stuck into the earth in the

center of the village. Near the pole sat drummers and singers
to supply the music for the dancers who formed up, men
facing women, ready to celebrate.

Among the other rights won by Long Walker was that of
Piane'epai'i, the Big Whip. At a Victory Dance he carried
his whip, its wooden handle having a serrated edge and
bearing symbols which represented his great deeds and two
short lashes of otter skin swinging free. The whip signified
that he acted as a kind of master of ceremonies and anybody
to whom he pointed must rise and dance, or be whipped. At
various times during the dance, the Big Whip had to halt the
music and relate a great deed performed by himself, ending
it with a sacred oath attesting the truth of his words.

"Sun, Father, you saw me do it. Earth, Mother, you saw
me do it. Do not let me live another season if I speak with a
forked tongue."

Should a warrior not wish to dance when called by the
Big Whip, he had the right to rise and tell his greatest deed.
If the crowd decided the deed was stronger than that of the
Big Whip, its teller need not dance. To gain the title of Big
Whip, a man must be the bravest of the brave; so his deeds
could rarely be bettered.

In the case of a major victory, or return of a very successful raiding party, the ensuing Victory Dance might continue
for several days. The fight that morning did not merit such
lengthy celebrations and it broke up soon after midnight.
However, before it ended Long Walker announced that
Loncey would be given his second Give-Away Dance as a
reward for rescuing his friend during the attack.

Much comment greeted the words, but everybody agreed
that the boy merited the honor. Never before had any Comanche received two Give-Away Dances at so young an age.
Clearly Loncey would be a name warrior and a pride to the
Pehnane if he continued to show such courage and ability.

Not to be outdone, Loud Voice and Comes For Food's
parents also announced a Give-Away Dance. For convenience's sake, the three celebrations were held on the same

night and acclaimed a great success. Each of the boys received, among other things, a good horse and a saddle. The latter gift caused much puffing out of young chests and delighted grins. Usually a boy rode bareback or on a blanket until old enough to ride in his first buffalo hunt, which normally preceded being taken on the warpath; but public opinion demanded special awards for the trio's courage.

One prize came Loncey's way at the Give-Away Dance. Hearing of Loncey's exploits, Sam Ysabel declared it to be time his son possessed a man's weapon. Among other items brought back from the trip was a Tryon, Son and Co. Mississippi rifle. At the height of the dance, Ysabel brought the rifle forward and presented it to his son along with a powder flask and bullet pouch. Despite the fact that the rifle had a length of four feet, one inch, and a caliber of .54, Loncey did not feel worried. Hefting the rifle in his hands, looking at its fine walnut stock and foregrip, the iron ramrod under the barrel and the patch box in the butt, he grinned like to split his face.

"How'd you like it, boy?" asked Ysabel.

"I like it fine, *'ap*," enthused Loncey.

A grin split the big white man's face and he winked at Long Walker. "Now all you have to do is learn to shoot with it, Loncey."

"If he's his father's son, that won't be hard for him," prophesied Long Walker.

In view of the way things would turn out, the chief made a mighty shrewd guess.

9

A Chance to Return a Gift

Although it tested his young muscles severely, Loncey quickly came to master the rifle. Coming from Kentuckian stock on his father's side, he appeared to inherit that rifle-toting breed's ability to aim true. Even quicker than accuracy came the ability to care for, clean and prepare the rifle to be fired. Although paper cartridges might be popular among the white settlers, Loncey knew nothing of them in early days. Instead he poured the powder charge direct from the horn, its built-in measure preventing him from using too many grains, and patch-loaded the bullet.

Nobody knows for sure who first discovered patch loading. The old-time woodsmen discovered that the European system of tapping home a bullet with a mallet down the rifle barrel could not be practiced in a country where keen-eared enemies lurked for the slightest sound. It was discovered that by casting the ball about a three-hundredths of an inch smaller than the rifle's bore and placing it upon a piece of

dressed buckskin, or felt, well soaked in tallow, a ramrod
could force the charge down the rifling lands of the barrel in
silence and ease. Nor did accuracy suffer, as the patch fitted
tightly into the rifling and formed a gastight seal without the
actual bullet being distorted. Using the patch method,
Loncey could soon get off two shots a minute, not a bad time
when one must pour in the powder, place patch and ball in
position and ram them home the full length of the iron rod,
then fit a percussion cap on the breech nipple. While practicing the loading, either so as to shoot, or dry, the boy longed
for a weapon which would fire several times without needing
to reload after each shot.*

Gaining accuracy took more time than learning the loading drill, but Ysabel saw to it that Loncey had access to a
good supply of powder and lead. The boy learned how to
mold his own bullets. When shooting, he quickly acquired
the knack of aligning the tip of the foresight in the center of
the target and squarely in the middle of the V-notch of the
backsight. Allowing for wind and trajectory of the bullet,
once taught, became almost a natural thing. Before two
months passed, Loncey could make consistent hits on a stationary *Aritsi* target at a hundred yards.

Not all his time went in rifle practice. The acquisition of a
saddle—made by a *tsukup* and resembling the modified
Spanish pattern most often seen by the Comanches—laid
open a whole new world of exciting horsemanship. Many of
the feats performed by warriors, such as hanging along the
racing horse's flank and discharging arrows or a bullet under its neck, could not be done when riding bareback. Once
given the security of a saddle, Loncey, Loud Voice and
Comes For Food swiftly mastered every trick, although they
all collected a few bruises and bumps in the process.

As mastery of saddle and rifle came, Loncey began to look
for an opportunity to repay his father for the latter gift. He
also hoped he might again perform an act which brought

---

* How Loncey achieved his ambition is told in *The Ysabel Kid.*

him into the limelight. The chance came one evening as he sat by Long Walker's fire, eating a meal and listening to Ysabel and the chief discussing the merits of various animals as food.

"There's nothing I like more than a taste of those wild bighorn sheep you get over in the high country to the west," Ysabel stated, after deer, elk, bear and antelope had been mentioned. "I'd sure admire to taste some again."

Listening to the word, Loncey began to form an idea. After finishing eating, he rose and went to find his two companions. In the way of his people, Loncey stated that he intended to ride on an expedition and wanted friends to go along with him. Without asking what Loncey planned, Loud Voice and Comes For Food offered their services. They showed no apprehension when hearing that Loncey meant to visit the distant hill country in search of a bighorn sheep to present to his father. Considering that from past performance, Loncey possessed the medicine power to succeed, his friends willingly put themselves under his orders.

"I'll bring pemmican for us," Loncey promised.

"We can use my pony as a packhorse," Comes For Food offered.

"My mother has plenty of jerked meat we can use," Loud Voice continued. "Will you be taking your bow, Loncey?"

"No. The rifle. How about you?"

His companions had no firearms and so said they would each bring his bow and arrows. From what Loncey had heard at various times, the rifle would be more suitable while hunting sheep. Although the bighorn sheep at that time had not been pushed into the most inaccessible crags by hunting pressure, they lived in country that did not lend itself to close-range stalking. So, despite it being slower to reload, Loncey settled on the rifle for the hunt.

At dawn the following morning, the boys headed for the remuda. After loading Comes For Food's pony with a few necessities, they caught and saddled their horses, then rode off to the west. Nobody questioned their right to go, nor would have raised any objections even if knowing they planned the one hundred and fifty mile trip to the western edge of the *Pehnane* country in search of bighorn sheep. If they were to be of any use to the community, young Comanches must show self-reliance, spirit and initiative. Preventing them from doing so had never been the Comanche way. Any boy who could not survive away from the village without adult supervision's education had been neglected and he would never make the grade as a warrior.

Despite the length of the journey, none of the trio felt at all worried. Their whole life's training had equipped them for just such an adventure. While expecting to live off the country, their pack pony carried parfleche bags—known as *awyaw: t* among the People—containing jerked meat and pemmican, both of which kept well and proved most welcome when fresh food could not be obtained. Jerked meat, usually sun-dried flesh of the buffalo, did not look appetizing but was nourishing. On the other hand, pemmican took more making, looked better and proved even more satisfactory to eat. After dried meat had been softened over a fire, berries, cherries, plums, piñon, pecan, walnuts, chestnuts or occasionally acorns, also partially dried and crushed, went into it. Stored in either an *awyaw: t* or the large intestine of a buffalo and coated in tallow to form an airtight seal, pemmican stayed fit to eat for a long period. Not that it often had a chance to put its fresh-keeping qualities to a test, being regarded among the People as a prime delicacy. Comanche children ate it sliced and coated in honey, enjoying every succulent mouthful.

To a Comanche on a journey, fifty miles a day constituted a reasonable pace. Filled with the eagerness of youth, the boys pushed their wiry horses a good fifty-five miles upon the first day. They traversed the range with an inborn sense of direction every member of the *Nemenuh* possessed, and with that same fixity of purpose that drove them as small children to spend an entire day if necessary in the pursuit of one particular hummingbird when hunting with the small bows and blunt arrows.

Toward evening Comes For Food and Loud Voice killed three jackrabbits with their bows. These served to give bulk and fresh meat to a meal that included the tuberous roots of the Indian potato, eaten raw, a few wild onions and bulbs of a sego lily. All in all the boys fared very well in the food line. Nor did they forget to take the basic precautions and made their camp in a small, wood-surrounded canyon which hid them and masked the light of their fire.

Another day's hard riding saw a further fifty miles behind them without incident. Traveling through the traditional hunting grounds of the *Pehnane,* they saw no sign of enemies. Next day the boys wended their way upward, through the wooded slopes, and toward evening made a well-concealed camp among the trees just below the open moorland on which the sheep lived.

In a few years' time, with the coming of the white man, the sheep would be hunted to the verge of extinction and pushed beyond the New Mexico line into the arid, semidesert hill country. However, when Loncey—possibly one of the first white men to enter and hunt the area—arrived with his two companions, the bighorn sheep still grazed in fair numbers in the high country beyond the timberline.

Finding sheep country proved far, far easier than making the required kill. With the cheery optimism of youth, the boys expected to arrive and, after a night's sleep, bag a sheep in the early morning, then return to the village in triumph and receive the plaudits of the people.

Their early training caused them to once more make a safe camp. Up in the high country among the spruce and jack pine, close to a stream, the boys tethered their horses and prepared to settle down. While Comes For Food went out to see what he could shoot for their meal, the other two collected wood and made a fire. When the sun went down, they found a decided chill in the air and so prepared to keep their fire going all night with as little inconvenience to themselves as possible. Taking the axe which Loud Voice remembered to bring along, Loncey cut two long, stout young saplings and took them to the camp. While he sank the saplings into the ground at an angle, Loud Voice brought in a number of logs from which the boys trimmed all branches and protuberances. After the fire had been lit and before going to sleep for the night, the boys placed the logs onto the sloping saplings so that the lowest rested upon the flames. While the boys slept in their buckskin shirts, breechclouts, leggings and moccasins, wrapped in a blanket each, the fire burned away the first log and the next rolled down into its place. While the system did not work perfectly, it saved the boys from spending too much sleeping time awake and tending the fire.

Dawn found the trio riding their horses over the open high country in search of their quarry. Although they found plenty of tracks and scats, noon came and went before the boys saw a flock of sheep. On seeing the animals, from a distance of at least a mile, and realizing what they must be, Loncey's party acted as they would when hunting whitetail deer. Retreating down a slope out of sight, they prepared to leave the horses and make a stalk. Then came the first lesson in a major difference between sheep and deer hunting. Loncey peeked back cautiously over the slope and saw, to his annoyance, the flock bounding away over a distant rim.

The previous night, seated around the campfire, Loncey and his friends had pooled their knowledge of sheep hunting. It came secondhand, from listening to fathers, uncles and elder brothers discussing the difficulties and techniques of the business. Their knowledge proved limited, for the Comanche—a realist and hunting meat, not sport—rarely went to the trouble necessary to hunt the sheep. About all the boys really knew was that any hunting must be done from a long range.

During the first day, the boys found that getting close enough for Loncey to chance a shot was next to impossible. Four more times during the day, the boys saw sheep without

being able to approach close enough for Loncey to use his
rifle. Among the keenest-sighted animals, the sheep also possessed good ears and a sharp nose. In addition, they did not
behave like the woodland game the boys usually hunted.

"They don't act like deer," Loncey stated as he sat with
his companions by the fire that night. "If you frighten a
deer, it will run a short way and then stop to see if you
follow."

"The sheep have strong medicine," admitted Loud Voice.
"When they see you, they run away and keep going."

That had been discovered when the boys tried tracking
the third flock they saw. After almost three miles, the sheep
had still been going and the trail petered out on a shale bank
which held no sign.

Determined to succeed, Loncey refused to think of giving
up the attempt, even though he realized that he faced a task
which might have tried the skill and knowledge of much
older, more experienced hunters than his party. Making the
camp their base, he started to sweep the high country. For
four days the boys hunted without success, but learned lessons from their failures. Normal deer-style stalking proved
useless. In each case the sheep saw the boys long before
human eyes located them and as soon as the boys took cover
to make their stalk, the sheep headed for safety. Due to the
bighorns' habit of keeping going once scared, tracking
brought no better result.

On the third day of their stay, Loncey began to get an
uneasy feeling of being watched. In later years he would
come to know that feeling and, relying on it, save his life
from hidden enemies.* While unable to shake the feeling, he
failed to see any sign of watchers and so said nothing of his
suspicions to his friends.

Remembering his grandfather's frequent advice about
turning an animal's habits to his advantage, Loncey gave
long and hard thought to the way the bighorns behaved.

* One occasion is told in *Apache Rampage*.

One significant point struck him early on the fourth day, causing him to halt his horse and look at his friends.

"The sheep always see us before we see them. Yet they don't run away as soon as we come into sight," he said. "They stand and watch us—"

"Until we hide from them," Loud Voice finished for him. "Then they run."

About an hour later the boys saw a flock of sheep higher up the hills and a mile away. Already the sheep had spotted them and stood staring in their direction.

"Let's stop and see what happens," Loncey suggested. "We'll stay in sight."

Obedient, as warriors should be when their leader gives an order, the other two halted their horses. Patiently they remained in the same place for over an hour and the sheep made no attempt to flee. Some of the flock resumed their feeding, two or three lying down, but always at least one watched the boys.

"Now we'll go out of sight," Loncey ordered after waiting for some sign of flight.

Not until the boys backed their mounts out of sight did the sheep turn and flee. Loncey felt that he might be approaching an answer to the problem. On the next contact with a flock, he continued to ride closer. Although he and his friends kept in plain sight, the sheep fled long before they reached shooting range.

"We could try riding them down, like buffalo," Comes For Food remarked.

"Over this sort of country?" Loncey scoffed. "No, that's not the answer. But I think I know what is."

"What?" asked his friends together.

"I'll tell you about it on the way back to the camp."

While riding back, Loncey explained his theory and the other two agreed that he might have hit upon the answer. More than ever Loncey felt the uneasy sensation of being watched. Halting his horse, he turned in the saddle and slowly scanned every inch of the country around him, but

without result. It seemed that neither of his companions had
yet developed the instinct, for they showed no concern and
took his action to mean that he sought for a sight of the
sheep.

At the camp, Loncey helped Comes For Food to prepare
for the night and Loud Voice went out in search of food.
However, they had been in the area for long enough to make
the animals wary and that night, for the first time, the boys
found themselves living on the rations brought from the village. Loncey knew that if his plan failed, he must call off the
expedition and return, for it would be a sign that his medicine was bad. No leader had the right to command under
such conditions. That night, after the other two went to
sleep, Loncey sat by the fire and said a silent prayer to *Ka-
Dih* that he might have success the following day.

Not until noon did they find what they wanted. It almost
appears that *Ka-Dih* looked with favor on the boy, for the
sheep—a flock of half a dozen rams—lay resting after feeding. Being on good grazing, the rams did not offer to leave
although all stood up as they caught sight of the boys in the
distance. Age-old instinct kept the sheep stationary. Their
natural enemies, bear, wolf and the occasional cougar,
hunted by stalking. When the sheep saw a predator, they
studied its actions. If it turned back into cover on seeing
them, they realized that it probably tried to stalk them and
so fled. When the predator remained in plain view, the sheep
did not worry until it came closer and could become a danger. While not being sure what the boys might be, the sheep
treated them as predators. Unconsciously Loncey hit upon
the answer to the sheep's tactics.

At about three quarters of a mile from the flock, Loncey
gave the order to halt the horses. He would have liked to go
closer, but decided not to chance doing so. Too much depended on his making a success of his scheme.

"This is our chance," he told the other two. "If it fails,
we'll go home."

"May *Ka-Dih* give you luck, brother," Loud Voice answered.

Following the plan thought out, Loncey eased himself backward out of the saddle. He moved slowly, sliding over the horse's rump and keeping its body between himself and the sheep. Hardly daring to breathe, he stood still until Loud Voice told him that the sheep showed no signs of departing.

"I'll see if I can get up to them then," Loncey said.

Cautiously he backed away from the horses, sinking to the ground with his rifle resting upon his arms. All the skill gained during his formative years went into locating the best route over which to make his stalk. Due to the nature of the ground he had to make a long detour. Taking advantage of every scrap of cover, using each rock and fold in the ground, Loncey swung around in a rough half-circle that he hoped would bring him up close to the sheep for him to chance a shot.

At one stage he crawled almost an inch at a time, flat on his belly and ignoring the pain as rocks jabbed into his flesh through the buckskins, across some twenty yards of open ground as there was no available cover. Just as he felt sure the sheep must see him, a narrow crack in the ground appeared. Rolling over its lip, he advanced in comparative ease and safety for some distance. Further along, the only way led him across a narrow ledge with a sheer, fifty-foot drop to jagged rocks if he missed his step.

Eventually he reached a point where he could see his two companions. They still sat their horses in the same place that he left them, a sure sign that the sheep had not moved. Reaching a group of rocks, he peered cautiously around them and his heart missed a beat. Not seventy-five yards from where he lay, the flock of sheep still studied the two boys and three horses.

In later years a shot at that range would have been simple enough; but at that early age it seemed like a great challenge. With infinite patience he slid the rifle forward be-

tween two of the rocks and snuggled down into a firing
position. Cuddling the butt to his shoulder, he sighted at the
nearest sheep, a young ram standing broadside onto his position. The rest of the flock lay down, watching the decoys,
but Loncey felt the standing sheep offered him the best
mark. Just as when he first aimed his bow at a deer, Loncey
felt a wave of buck fever hit him and the rifle's barrel wavered instead of lining steadily. Sucking in his breath, he
forced himself to be calm and took a careful aim at just
behind the ram's shoulder.

When sure of his aim, Loncey held his breath and
squeezed the trigger. Never had the big side hammer appeared to move so slowly as at that moment. It seemed to
creep down at a snail's pace before it finally struck the cop-
per head of the waiting percussion cap. After the faint pop
of the cap's fulminate charge, what seemed like several minutes elapsed before the powder in the barrel exploded and its
gas sent the bullet spitting from the barrel.

Flame finally spurted from the barrel and a cloud of black
powder smoke momentarily hid the sheep from the boy's
view. Although the Mississippi rifle packed a fair kick—
Loncey did not use a benchrest shooter's extreme care in
ensuring the charge of powder remained constant at each
loading—the boy hardly felt its savage jab.

Then the smoke cleared and through it Loncey saw a
sheep disappearing over the rim above him. Only for a minute did fear and disappointment bite at him. The remainder
of the smoke wafted away and he saw something lying on
the ground. Loud in the still air rang his wild whoop of
delight at the sight of the ram sprawled before him.

Just as Loncey started to rise, meaning to dash forward
and examine his prize, he remembered his experience upon
his first hunt. With hands that shook a little, he reloaded
and capped the rifle. Not until he held a usable weapon did
he advance toward the sheep. By that time his two companions had started the horses moving and rode as fast as they
dared in his direction.

"You did it, Loncey," enthused Loud Voice, dropping from his horse and looking down at the dead ram.

"What a shot," Comes For Food went on excitedly. "It never moved after it fell."

"That was because the bullet broke its neck," Loud Voice pointed out. "Loncey shot it there so as not to waste the better parts of the meat."

Loncey coughed modestly and did not offer to mention that he actually aimed at the ram's body.

10

A Present for Sam Ysabel

With the kill made, the boys went to work at butchering the carcass. Loncey allowed the other two to share the gall-soaked liver between them as a reward for their companionship. Even at so early an age, he knew how a name warrior must act. In return Loud Voice and Comes For Food performed most of the butchering and left Loncey free to scan the surrounding area. Making the meat up into three equal bundles, the boys carried the sheep's hide. They left behind the head, having split it open to feast on the brains. The Comanche had no use for horns as a mere trophy and the pack pony would be carrying enough without added, useless weight.

Once again the boys' inborn instinct pointed them in the correct direction. When they reached the rolling plains, landmarks noted on the way out would guide them back to the village. If their people had moved on during their ab-

sence, any one of the trio could read sign and follow the trail
to the next campsite.

Having nothing more to hold them in the high country,
and wanting to return to the warmth of the plains, the boys
broke camp instead of staying for the night.

"I kept thinking we were being watched all day," Comes
For Food commented as he reached for the packhorse's
reins.

"So have I," admitted Loud Voice, "but I've seen no sign
of watchers."

"We are close to Apache country," Loncey reminded the
others. "But, if they were Apaches watching, they have not
come close."

For all that the boys rode on until well after dark and
made a fireless camp. Next day they continued the journey
and toward evening found themselves traveling through broken, wooded country. All kept a careful watch through the
day without seeing any sign of danger. Coming from the
wooded land, they approached a wide, gentle-sided valley.

"Look!" Loud Voice hissed, pointing.

A party of riders came into sight on the other side of the
valley; four stocky Indian braves, all well armed, a tallish,
slender woman and a boy of about the trio's age, the latter
couple each leading a pair of laden packhorses.

On observing the boys, the other party came to a halt and
the braves reached for their weapons. Having the width of
the valley between them, the boys saw no reason for immediate flight, especially when the braves did not carry rifles
and sat beyond arrow shot.

Clearly the braves decided there was no danger to themselves. Moving his horse forward, the oldest man made an
unmistakable signal in the sign language all Plains Indians
understood. Loncey raised his arm with the elbow bent and
right palm facing the ground. By moving the arm to the
right in a wriggling motion, he answered the request to be
informed which tribe the trio hailed from.

At some time in the distant past a party of the People

made a long journey in search of new hunting grounds. Not caring for the direction being taken, several members of the party insisted on turning back. Filled with indignation at the lack of faith in his ability, the chief who led them compared the dissidents to a snake backing up on its tracks. Since then the Comanche, no matter which band he came from, always used the sign of the "snake going backward" when given a signaled request for the name of his tribe.

"What tribe are you?" signaled Loncey, although he could guess, after announcing that he and his companions belonged to the People.

"Nemenuh," grunted Loud Voice when the brave confirmed their suspicions by repeating Loncey's sign. "The men are of the People, but not the woman."

"She may be the *pairaivo* of one of the braves," Loud Voice remarked. "She's a Mexican, I'd say."

Apparently the other party accepted the boys' *bona fides,* for they started to ride down into the valley and toward the trio. Not to be outdone in courtesy, Loncey led his companions to meet the visitors to their country halfway.

"The braves wear antelope skins," he said. "They must be from the *Kweharehnuh* coming to visit us."

As he spoke, Loncey studied the approaching riders. The men looked much the same as warriors from the *Pehnane* village, except that most of their clothing came from the pronghorn antelope instead of the buckskin favored, being more accessible, by the Wasps.

From the braves, his eyes went to the woman. Like Loud Voice remarked, no Comanche woman, she was taller and slimmer, with less Mongoloid features than one of the *Nemenuh.* Most likely a Mexican captive taken as wife by one of the warriors; such often happened, Loncey guessed. He might have thought of her as still retaining signs of beauty had he been older, but at twelve gave little thought to such unimportant matters.

The boy would be the woman's son if appearances meant anything. Stocky, typical Antelope Comanche in dress, his

features held a sullen expression that would twist into real
savage cruelty when older. Clearly he was a favorite son, or
had performed powerful deeds, for a good knife hung at his
belt and he carried one of the wood and elkhorn compound
bows preferred by the *Kweharehnuh,* living as they did in
country which held few trees. The boy sat in the saddle of a
good horse and eyed the approaching trio with as much
interest as they studied him.

"Who are you?" demanded the leading brave, speaking
fluent Comanche, but with a quicker inflection than a
Pehnane gave his words.

"We are from the Quick Stingers," Loncey replied.
"These are Comes For Food and my brother, Loud Voice."

"And who are you?" asked the woman.

That came as something of a surprise and caused Loncey
to revise his opinion as to the woman's status. No mere wife
would dare to intervene at such a moment. In fact only a
medicine woman of some power would do so.

"My name is Loncey," he said.

"You are not Comanche," the woman went on.

"My father is Ysabel, of the Dog Soldier lodge," Loncey
explained. "And my grandfather is one called Long
Walker."

He could see that the latter name impressed the Antelope
braves. However, the woman gave no sign of knowing the
name of the *Pehnane* war chief. Instead she sat her horse
and glowered at him with dark eyes which held a hint of
something he could not understand. Young as he was,
Loncey read the hate that flickered across the woman's face
at the mention of his father and grandfather, yet he could
not explain it. The woman might be a captive but that did
not necessarily mean she suffered torture at her captor's
hands. Being a realist, the Comanche rarely wasted time
inflicting punishment that might kill or injure a useful piece
of property. It had never been Long Walker's way to do so
under any circumstances. If the woman had been a *Pehnane,*

an ancient feud might have caused her dislike; but she rode among a group of *Kweharehnuh.*

Although Loncey had heard of the death of Bitter Root, an unimportant detail like the feelings of the brave's Mexican-captive wife had been omitted. Maybe Loncey would have understood had he known the facts, and felt concern at his present position.

After long years among the *Kweharehnuh,* Fire Dancer was returning to the *Pehnane.* Following the line used in her second marriage, she insisted that each of her subsequent husbands announced his will on making her *pairaivo.* Of course snags arose when the other wives demanded a more even sharing of property than the dead man desired and in each case Fire Dancer failed to make the grand swoop she hoped for. However, four Antelope marriages, each ending in the sudden, mysterious death of the husband, gave her wealth. Considerable reluctance developed among the *Kweharehnuh* braves when word went out that once more Fire Dancer sought a husband. Finding no takers, Fire Dancer settled down to a widow's life, which did not prove too unpleasant as the braves saw that she never went hungry. She also made advances to the village's medicine woman and, at the cost of much property, learned various secrets. That had begun four years before and Fire Dancer might have succeeded her instructor when the other died had she not decided that she possessed the knowledge to extract vengeance on the man who killed her first husband.

Sitting her horse among the escort hired to guide her back to the *Pehnane* country, Fire Dancer glared at the tall, slim, handsome youngster. It seemed that the fates smiled on her, presenting her with such an early opportunity. Before her sat the son of the man she most hated, a favored son if his horse, saddle, knife and rifle be anything to go on. To cause the son's death would make a fitting start to her revenge on Sam Ysabel, especially as it had been the boy's birth which led to Bitter Root's death.

"I hear his thoughts," she told the men, staring at Loncey with cold, unwinking eyes. "He is—"

"Up there!" put in the youngest brave of the escort.

All eyes followed the direction of his gaze and studied the two men who sat their horses at the top of the slope down which the boys rode. Despite the unexpected appearance, none of the Antelope braves showed any sign of alarm. While one of the pair might be a big buckskin-clad white man, the rifle over his arm reposed in a Dog Soldier medicine sheath; the second was clearly a *Pehnane,* as showed by the shield on his arm and the powerful wood bow in his other hand.

"Ysabel!" breathed Fire Dancer, recognizing the white man, and wondered how she might turn the meeting to her advantage.

Before she could make any move, the Antelopes raised their hands in answer to the newcomers' peace sign and relaxed. Starting their horses moving, Ysabel and War Club rode toward the others. Loncey felt some relief, mingled with surprise, at seeing his father and foster father approaching when they ought to have been far off at the *Pehnane* village.

"Greetings," War Club said to the Antelope leader. "I am *Wepitapu'ni* of the *Pehnane* Dog Soldiers."

"I am one called Burnt Grass of the *Kweharehnuh.* With me are Raider, José and Hawk Circling. This medicine woman asked us to bring her to your village. She is Fire Dancer and the boy her son, No Father."

"They will be welcome among our people," War Club promised formally.

As a medicine woman, although originally a captive, Fire Dancer commanded respect from even a name warrior and she knew War Club told the truth. Seeing all chance of creating doubt as to the boy's identity gone, she accepted the situation. With an effort she masked the hate in her eyes and nodded gravely in answer to the *Pehnane*'s offer. Once es-

tablished at the village, she could take her time in arranging
her vengeance against all concerned in Bitter Root's death.

With the introductions completed, the combined party
started to move once more in the direction of the *Pehnane*
village. While making for a suitable campsite in which to
spend the night, War Club told the Antelopes of Loncey's
achievements. Showing as much pride as if the boy was his
own flesh and blood, the *Pehnane* described Loncey's defeat
of *"Piamempits"* and how he handled himself during the
Waco attack. Grins creased the faces of the Antelopes and
they praised the boy, being always ready to give credit where
it be due.

Bringing up the rear of the party, Loud Voice and Comes
For Food told No Father much the same story. Boastfully
the surly-faced youngster insisted that he had also performed great deeds, but acted evasive when questioned as to
what they might be. Nor would he accompany the others
when they swung away from the main body to see what food
they might bring in for the night's camp.

"I wonder what our father is doing out here, Loncey,"
Loud Voice asked as they rode away.

"Perhaps they went after sheep too," Comes For Food
suggested. "If they did, they couldn't have had good hunting."

Not until making camp for the night did Loncey learn the
reason for his father's presence. When the boys failed to
return to camp, Ysabel and War Club questioned some of
their friends. Considering the trio to be just a mite young for
such an extended trip, yet not wanting to curb their spirits,
the men took up the trail. On seeing how well the boys
conducted themselves, Ysabel and War Club decided to remain in the background and not make their presence
known. The meeting with the Antelope party brought them
into the open.

"We'd been watching you for three days, boy," Ysabel
told Loncey, speaking English. "You did good on that last
stalk, real good. Won me a good buffalo horse off War Club,

too. He said it'd take you another day at least to figure out how to get up close enough to drop a sheep."

"It wasn't easy," Loncey admitted. "I thought for three days that somebody watched us, but never saw a sign of you."

"That figures," drawled his father dryly. "We didn't aim to be seen. How'd you like to come down into Mexico with me next time I go, boy?"

"I'd like it fine, *'ap,*" the boy enthused, for such a trip had all the glory of a raiding expedition due to the prevailing conditions.

With feelings against Mexico still running high as a result of the war, and possibly seeking a more profitable source of revenue than the indifferent taxes paid by the Texans, the U.S. Government tried to impose import or export duty upon all goods trafficked across the international border. Although originally sent to Texas as a law-enforcement and protective body, many U.S. troops found themselves engaged in the attempts to enforce the tariffs. That left the way clear for Indian depredations and brought much hostility from the Texans, who had disbanded the Rangers—a highly efficient Indian-fighting force—and found themselves left unprotected.

Regarding their neighbors to the north in no better light, the Mexican Government also tried to impose customs duties upon people trading across the Rio Grande. Between them, despite the length of the area to be covered, the two governments managed to make trading—or smuggling as it soon became—a decidedly risky pastime for the men involved in it.

Smuggling became highly profitable also, as legislative prohibition invariably creates a demand for the banned items. People on both sides of the border suddenly decided that they could not exist without certain items obtainable only in the other country. All that remained was to find somebody willing to supply their needs—and there has

never been a commodity that could not be bought or supplied, law or no law, if the price be right.

To men like Sam Ysabel a thing like customs duties bore
all the intolerable stench of an infringement of personal lib-
erty. Having traded across the border from the days when
Texas was a republic, he saw no reason why some fat Yankee
politician shining his butt-end on a chair in Austin—or far-
off Washington—should interfere. So Ysabel turned from
trader to smuggler, running goods across the border and
defying the U.S. or Mexican army to stop him. As yet he
operated in a small way, but sensed the day must come when
he would be forced to make it his living.

Already Ysabel could see the way things headed in Texas.
Since the transition to statehood gave the chance of stability
and security, many settlers began to pour in from the north
and east. As yet the influx made but little impression on the
vast area of the state, but Ysabel knew it would eventually.
Farseeing men like the Hardin, Fog and Blaze clan on their
vast Rio Hondo holdings, Big Rance Counter down in the
Big Bend and Charles Goodnight up in the Panhandle country saw the possibilities of Texas' untold miles of rich grass-
land. They began to breed cattle, turning the long-horned
stock of Mexican origin loose to fend untended on the range
and building the nucleus of the great herds which would
mean so much to the fate of the Lone Star State in the
future.

Gradually, but surely, the ranches expanded and grew in
numbers, pushing ever closer to Comancheria. Soon the cat-
tlemen would be approaching the *Pehnane* country and
Ysabel knew what the outcome must be. Buffalo and cattle
could not share the same range in the numbers that used it
at that time. So the buffalo would have to go, and upon them
the Indian depended. Sooner or later the *Pehnane* must
adopt a different mode of life. Ysabel knew the futility of his
friends trying to fight against the inevitable and hoped they
would not try.

Being a realist, Ysabel knew he would need a trade when the change came. One could not treat another man's cattle as if they were buffalo, deer or antelope—not without considerable shooting fuss developing—so some other way of obtaining food must be found.

Smuggling offered Ysabel a damned good way, while being as close as a man could come to retaining the good, free old *Pehnane* life. Not that he aimed to teach Loncey the business so young, but he figured his son deserved a trip and had reached the age when he ought to be seeing how white folks lived.

"Get some sleep, boy," he ordered. "We'll talk about it some more when we get back to the village."

After Loncey settled down for the night, Ysabel threw a glance across to where Fire Dancer lay under her blankets. He wondered what brought the woman back to the *Pehnane* country after so many years among the *Kweharehnuh*. If the occasional rumors which filtered through from the Antelope country be true, she seemed mighty unlucky in keeping a husband. Likely she could not find any more men willing to chance marrying her and came back to the *Pehnane* in the hope of— No, Burnt Grass called her a medicine woman. Could it be that she came back to meet Raccoon Talker and learn a few things about her business?

Although pretending to be asleep, Fire Dancer sensed Ysabel's eyes on her. All the hate stored up for so many years beat inside her and she looked toward the packs at the edge of the camp. In one of them lay a suitable present for Sam Ysabel. She wondered if she should use it right then. After a moment's thought, she discarded the idea. Even if successful, she knew that the attempt could be too easily traced back to her. The Comanche would have no mercy upon her when caught taking that kind of revenge. So she decided to wait until a more suitable moment.

Having reached her decision, Fire Dancer closed her eyes

and went to sleep. Unaware of the plans Fire Dancer made
for ending his future, Ysabel made up the fire and then
rolled into his blankets, settling down easily upon the only
kind of bed he ever felt really comfortable when using.

11

The Gift That Went Astray

Much to his disappointment, Loncey found his triumphant return overshadowed by the fact that a raiding party had returned earlier after a most successful trip down into Mexico. However, Loncey admitted that his exploit, important as it might be to him did not compare with the achievements of the raiding party. His grandfather praised him and Ysabel promised to tell of the successful hunt during the later stages of the celebrations.

One major difference showed in the Victory Dance for the raiding party and that held to celebrate the defeat of the Wacos. Around the scalp pole, with its hanging trophies, sat half a dozen scared Mexican children bound hand and foot, and much of the party's loot was set out close by so that all might see how well the braves did during the raid. Much the same songs rolled out, drums beating out rhythm, and dancers performing the steps in the flickering light of the flames. At first the voices kept low and held the tempo down, but gradually it swelled in volume and the pace built up. Frequently one of the party left the dancing line, approaching the prisoners and pretending to kill then scalp the Mexicans. No lives had been lost on the raid, so nothing beyond pretense happened to the bound group by the scalp pole.

In one way Fire Dancer felt pleased to have arrived at such an opportune moment. Due to excitement at the forthcoming celebrations, nobody troubled to question her reason for returning. A brave from the raiding party, flushed with success, presented her with a tepee and some cooking utensils. Beyond that, she found herself practically ignored as people prepared for the dance. Womanlike, the disinterest annoyed her at first. Then she saw that it improved her chances of dealing with Ysabel and avoiding coming under suspicion.

With typical Comanche hospitality, the Antelope braves were welcomed and invited to attend the dance. After the leader of the successful raiders had told his story, Long Walker danced over to Burnt Grass and, in his capacity of Big Whip, acted in the traditional manner. Knowing what was expected of him, Burnt Grass rose and declined to dance. Instead he told the story of his greatest coup, how he stole a number of horses from under the noses of a U.S. Dragoon company, evading the sentries, cutting a picket line and leading animal after animal away without being detected. When the story ended, Long Walker indicated that Burnt Grass could sit down as no exploit of his own could equal the deed. Not to be outdone in courtesy, the Antelope chief joined the dancing. In that way honor was satisfied all round and nobody's feelings hurt by having to rate the merit of one deed against another.

As the evening went on, the dance's pace increased. When sure that nobody would notice them, or form the wrong opinion if they did, Fire Dancer led José, the youngest member of her escort, into darkness.

"What is it, medicine woman?" he inquired a touch impatiently, having been making satisfactory progress with a pretty *Pehnane naivi* and not caring for the interruption.

"I have something for you to do," Fire Dancer answered.

"What is it?"

"I want you to take this *awyaw: t* of pemmican to the tepee of the one called Ysabel and leave it inside."

The young Antelope brave showed no surprise at Fire Dancer's suggestion. Often a middle-aged widow took such a way of showing an older man that she would be willing to contemplate matrimony. Sending a sample of her cooking to the intended's tepee allowed him to decide how well she might be able to tend to his needs. Pemmican, being regarded as such a delicacy, was the most frequent choice for such a gift.

"Where do I find this tepee?" asked José.

"Over there by Long Walker's," answered the woman. "It is the one with the grulla stallion tethered close by."

Again the brave saw nothing unusual. A woman sending somebody on that sort of delicate mission would make certain that she supplied information to guide the messenger to the right tepee.

"Will there be anybody in the tepee?" José asked, taking the *awyaw: t* from the woman.

"Ysabel has no woman, as I have discovered. Both he and his son are by the fire and the tepee will be empty."

"Then I will go now."

"Let no one see what you are doing," warned Fire Dancer grimly, "and say nothing of it to anybody."

"Nobody but Ysabel will know," José promised.

"See that they don't!" hissed the woman and returned to the fire.

José frowned. While he did not care to have a woman address him in such a manner, he recollected that Fire Dancer had certain medicine power. In view of the high mortality rate of her husbands, that power had best not be angered. So he held down his feelings, resolved to maintain strict silence about his mission, and set off to complete it.

On leaving the fire, José made a circle into the darkness and behind the tepees as he headed for Ysabel's dwelling. Several of the inevitable cur-dogs to be found in any Comanche village roamed in the darkness, but they recognized Indian scent and made no fuss.

Despite having been lavishly entertained, José still felt a little peckish and eyed the *awyaw: t* speculatively. Much to his delight, he noticed that the end had already been opened and slices removed. Most likely Ysabel would not miss another wedge; and, after all, José figured he deserved some reward for wasting time that could have been profitably spent in the company of the *naivi.* Halting in the darkness, he drew back the outer covering from the pemmican. With his knife, he sliced off a piece of Ysabel's gift. José continued on his way. He found the tepee with no difficulty and halted outside. While everybody seemed to be around the main fire and engrossed in the entertainment, he knew better than to take the chance of being seen entering an unoccupied tepee. Deciding that the white man probably followed the *Nemenuh* way of placing his bed so it faced the tepee's entrance, José solved his problem in a simple manner. He tossed the pemmican through the door, heard it thud gently on its arrival, and returned to the fire. Catching Fire Dancer's eye, José nodded to show her that he had carried out her orders.

Much to Fire Dancer's annoyance, Ysabel did not offer to return to his tepee. Like all his kind, Ysabel liked to buckle in and really enjoy himself given the opportunity. So he remained by the fire, joining in the dancing, eating and generally enjoying himself. Nor did the woman's second hope evolve, for Loncey did not visit the tepee either. Like most of the younger boys, he soon grew tired of the celebrations around the fire. Gathering his companions, he faded off into the night, meaning to play at the old Comanche game of stealing horses.

One of the half-starved cur-dogs, catching the scent of the pemmican, halted outside Ysabel's tepee. Hunger caused it

to approach the door. Cautiously, ready to leap back and
flee, the dog entered the tepee. It darted across to Ysabel's
bed, snatched up the *awyaw: t* in its jaws and ran back out of
the door. Drawing off into the darkness, the dog began to
eat its prize and fight off the attempts of other curs which
came up. Some four of the dogs finally shared the pemmican
Fire Dancer intended for Sam Ysabel.

Toward midnight, by white man's time, José began to feel
uncomfortable. At first he took it to be no more than distress
caused by overloading his stomach with good food. Slowly
the pain increased, driving into his body and seeming to
knot his stomach. Suddenly he remembered Sam Ysabel's
gift. Maybe the medicine woman had put a curse on the
pemmican to prevent any but the man for who she intended
it enjoying the tasty present. Once again a knifelike thrust of
pain drove through his body and he lurched to his feet. Not
far away from him sat Ysabel. Maybe if he went to the white
man and confessed, the medicine would end.

"Ysa—bel—!" he gasped.

All eyes went to the young man. Clutching at his stomach, José took a couple of staggering strides toward the
white man. Even as Ysabel came to his feet, José tottered
and crashed face downward to the ground.

"What the hell?" demanded Ysabel, moving forward and
dropping to his knees alongside the writhing Antelope
brave.

Raccoon Talker left the place where she sat among the
other dignitaries of the village. The music stopped and every
eye turned in the direction of the groaning brave. Looking
up, Ysabel growled a warning to keep back and ended the
forward surge of curious people. After throwing a grateful
glance at the big white man, Raccoon Talker bent closer to
make an examination. After only a quick glance, she knew
that the brave lay far beyond her powers. From all the symp-
toms, the young man had been poisoned and she felt that she
could hazard a guess at the nature of the poison.

The knowledge puzzled Raccoon Talker for, if true, ev-

erything pointed to the poison being deliberately administered. Only a very young Comanche child would eat the
Deadly Amanita mushroom, being ignorant of its lethal nature. No grown man would knowingly consume it, being
taught early how to differentiate between edible and poisonous plants.

Given time and starting at the first warning sign, Raccoon
Talker might have been able to accomplish something. Before she could even ask for her medicine bag to be brought
along, the brave vomited violently, went into a convulsion of
tormented writhing and died.

Once again Raccoon Talker felt puzzled, knowing the
length of time required by the Deadly Amanita's poison to
take effect to be around fifteen hours after consumption.

"He is dead," she announced, looking up to where the
Antelope braves gathered in the forefront of the crowd.

"How did he die?" asked Burnt Grass.

"It looks to me as if he had been poisoned," Fire Dancer
put in.

Instantly the three remaining *Kweharehnuh* men moved
closer, throwing coldly suspicious glances around them.
Raider, José's elder brother, growled out the question which
passed through every mind.

"How did he come to take the poison?"

All eyes went to the group of people with whom José
spent most of the time. Rising, the father of the *naivi* who
attracted the young brave growled, "He ate nothing that we
did not."

"When did he eat before that?" Raccoon Talker continued.

"Not since sunup, I reckon," Ysabel answered. "We made
a good meal before we broke camp this morning and didn't
stop again until we reached the village."

That figured to anybody who knew the way of Comanches
on the last leg of a journey. Rising early, so as to cook a
meal then douse the fire before daylight allowed its smoke to
be seen, they pushed on until reaching their destination

without bothering to take more food. If José had eaten the poisonous mushrooms in the early hours of the dawn, their effects ought to have shown much sooner.

"This is strange," said the medicine woman, half to herself.

"You may use one of my tepees, Antelope brother," remarked the leader of the successful raiding party, making a typically generous gesture in presenting the bereaved men with a place in which to lay out their dead companion. "And I think we will dance no more this night."

"You have our thanks," Burnt Grass replied. "Come, Raider, I will help you carry your brother."

Grief twisted Raider's face and he glared around him. "I still want to know how J—he came to be poisoned."

Tactfully Burnt Grass smoothed over the implied insult and, assisted by Long Walker, Ysabel and the raiding party's leader, carried the dead brave to the supplied death tepee. There Burnt Grass persuaded Raider to leave the business of laying out the body to them. Turning, Raider passed through the tepee door. He stood for a moment glaring around suspiciously and then turned and stalked into the darkness.

While the dance had been canceled, excitement and interest ran too high for the people of the village to seek their beds. Instead they gathered about the big main fire, or in groups at family blazes and discussed the death of the *Kweharehnuh* visitor. One man, going into the darkness on a natural errand, stumbled over something and bent down. He found a dead dog, its body twisted in agony much as the Antelope brave's had been, but did not connect the two incidents. Growling a curse, he gripped the dog's legs and dragged it into the bushes. Little did he know that three more dogs lay dead in the vicinity, having devoured the pemmican which should have been left in Ysabel's tepee.

If anybody noticed that Fire Dancer followed Raider into the darkness, they thought nothing of it. Catching up with the man, she led him clear of the tepees and looked around to make sure that none of the *Pehnane* could overhear her words. While traveling from the *Kweharehnuh* country, she had come to know her escort pretty well. A medicine woman needed to be a shrewd judge of human nature, and Fire Dancer used her knowledge of Raider to further her own plans. Knowing how José came by the poison, she assumed that he had devoured some of the pemmican and hid the remainder to be consumed later. That meant her gift to Ysabel had gone astray, and she must use other means of settling accounts with the big white man. Typical of the way her mind worked, she decided to use the brother of her victim. José failed her, but had passed beyond punishment. So she intended to make his brother suffer for the dead brave's disobedience to her wishes.

"What do you want, medicine woman?" growled Raider. "This journey has been bad medicine. J— My brother is dead."

"That is why I come to you," Fire Dancer replied. "You know I have the power given by *Ka-Dih*?"

"So it is said."

"I have it—for do I not know who killed your brother?"

Interest showed on the dull, grief-lined face. Like all Comanches, Raider felt a strong bond with his younger brother. With José dead, murdered it seemed, Raider must take revenge upon the one responsible.

"Who?"

The word came in a hate-filled growl and Raider's blunt, powerful fingers closed upon the tomahawk in his belt. Watching the man intently, Fire Dancer knew that she could achieve her ends if she handled him the right way.

"Ysabel!" she spat out the name dramatically.

"Ysabel?" repeated the man, sounding puzzled. "Why would he do it?"

"He is a white man; and do not all white-eyes hate us?"

"But he lives among the *Pehnane*—"

"So that he can learn their secrets and betray them. Ask the people of the village how many braves ride out and never return; what women disappear without a trace; whose children have died mysteriously. They do not know who is behind all this, but I know. I have the power to read the hidden thoughts, so I know that Ysabel does all this."

Even as she spoke, Fire Dancer knew that Raider would not trouble to ask any questions among the people of the village. She knew enough about the man to guess at his reactions to her words. While a name warrior of some ability, Raider's fame rested on blind courage rather than tactical thought. Aware that Raider was not the most intelligent of men, she played on his grief and knew she could sway him to her will. Even so, the man did not take her words entirely for granted.

"Why did he kill my brother?"

"Because the dead one knew his secret and meant to tell the people."

"Then I will go and kill him!"

"Stop!" commanded the woman, catching Raider's arm. "Ysabel is no ordinary man and has medicine power to protect him. Nor will the *Pehnane* believe you if you speak of this, because of his medicine. Not even if you took the buffalo-chip oath to show you spoke the truth."

Among the Antelope band, no oath was so sacred as that taken over a pile of buffalo chips. If the *Pehnane* refused to accept testimony given upon such an oath, Ysabel must possess strong medicine. So Raider did as Fire Dancer expected, he asked for the assistance of one who also had medicine power.

"My brother cries for vengeance," he said.

"So I hear, for he has already spoken with me from the Land of Good Hunting."

"What did he say, medicine woman?" asked Raider, suitably impressed.

"That you must act in a certain manner. Only if you do can you break Ysabel's medicine and avoid being killed."

"Then how do I do it? I am a simple man. If I see an enemy, I kill him and that is all there is to it."

"You will go to Ysabel's tepee, which I can show you, and wait inside. He has no woman, but his son may be there. If so, kill the boy as silently as you would a horse-herd guard—"

"That I know well enough how to do," admitted Raider, having gained his man-name by an ability to steal horses.

"Kill the boy," continued Fire Dancer, ignoring the interruption. "And wait inside the tepee until Ysabel returns. Then strike him down in such a manner that he can't cry out. After he is dead, leave the tepee and make sure nobody sees you go."

"All that I can do," said Raider.

"Then do it as I said, or you will fail through Ysabel's medicine power. If you do as I told you, Ysabel will die and none know who killed him."

There might, Fire Dancer admitted to herself, be some suspicions when the villagers remembered how Ysabel killed her first husband. However she intended to spend the remainder of the night making medicine talk with Raccoon Talker and so be dissociated from the deed she planned.

Dull-witted Raider might be, but he grasped the necessary points of the plan easily enough and needed no repetition as Fire Dancer led him in the direction of Ysabel's tepee. Making sure the man knew exactly where to go, Fire Dancer parted company with him before coming too close to his destination and went to set about the business of establishing her alibi.

Approaching the tepee, Raider saw Ysabel's big grulla stallion standing picketed before its entrance. Had he been dealing with another Comanche, the sight would have worried him. Nothing Raider had seen in sporadic meetings with other white men led him to believe that they possessed any of the horse-training ability of the People. So he doubted if Ysabel would prove more adept, or that the grulla received the training instilled into a warrior's favorite horse.

With his tomahawk in hand, Raider glided silently up to the tepee. He paused in the shadows, keen ears listening for any sound to tell him that the tepee was occupied. Concentrating upon that, he completely failed to notice a change in the grulla's attitude; one which, if observed, might have changed his thoughts on the subject of white man's horse-training ability. Quickly he stepped into the tepee, raising the door flap only sufficiently to allow himself entrance room. The light of the big main fire, glowing in the background, momentarily lit up the tepee's interior. A couple of saddles lay upon their sides on the left of the door, ready to be grabbed up when leaving. At the far side were two beds, both empty, with a pair of rifles, a bow and quiver of arrows close to them All that Raider noticed as he entered. A feeling of disappointment hit him when he found that Ysabel's son was not present. Two lives would have been better payment for his brother's death.

Stepping to one side, he crouched in the darkness with the tomahawk in his hand. He expected a long wait, accepting it as part payment for being given an opportunity to avenge his brother's murder. So it came as a pleasant surprise, an omen almost, to hear the sound of approaching feet and see the tepee's door flap begin to lift.

With his head full of thoughts about Ysabel's medicine power, Raider decided not to take any chances. The moment that the person outside began to enter, he launched a savage chop designed to lay open the other's throat and prevent any outcry.

A day's hard riding followed by a sufficiency of good food since his return to the village did much to damp Loncey's usual enthusiasm for the game of stealing horses. Normally he would have spent most of the night with his friends, practicing how to rope a selected animal from a resting remuda and keep it silent while leading it away. After leaving the Victory Dance, he went with the other members of his band, but collected only one horse, galloping it around the village to test its mettle, then decided to go home. Dropping from the borrowed horse, he watched it rejoin the remuda and then walked back to the village.

When approaching puberty, a Comanche boy had to stay clear of his sisters. In most cases, that meant living in a separate tepee from the remainder of the family. Having no wife, or daughters, Ysabel could allow Loncey to share the tepee with him, so it was to his father's home that Loncey went on his return.

As he neared the tepee, Loncey glanced instinctively in the direction of his father's horse. What he saw brought him to a halt and caused the back hairs on his neck to rise in warning. Instead of resting, the stallion stood facing the tepee's door, its head held high and ears pricked in an alert manner. For a moment the boy stood undecided as to his best course of action. He knew the horse, like any warrior's favorite mount, had been trained to give warning of lurking danger. From the signs, something—or somebody—had recently entered the tepee and must still be inside.

If a human being was in the tepee, it must be an enemy. While the Comanche did not hesitate to appropriate an outsider's horse or property, they never stole from each other. Therefore the person in the tepee could not be a friend.

Just as Loncey prepared to turn and fetch help, a thought struck him. What if nothing more than a prowling cur-dog, raccoon or porcupine should be the cause of the horse's warning? Every brave act Loncey had performed would be forgotten and there were some who would be only too pleased to see him brought down to their level by making a foolish mistake. The thought of being a subject of mockery made up Loncey's mind for him. It would be better to take a chance than run for help to deal with an inoffensive, nondangerous animal.

Sliding the knife from his sheath, he walked up to the tepee and raised the door flap. Only for a moment did he hesitate, then, sucking in a breath, he entered. A movement from the right caught his attention. He saw a human shape lunge in his direction, its arm lashing around toward him. Instantly he flung himself forward in a rolling dive and heard the hiss of a weapon passing harmlessly over his head.

Three things saved the boy's life: first, he expected danger and was ready for it; secondly, he moved with considerable speed; lastly, Raider assumed the one entering to be Sam Ysabel and aimed his tomahawk at a height to slash the white man's throat open, preventing any outcry, so it passed over the level of the boy's head.

Snarling in rage, Raider caught his balance, whirled around and charged across the tepee in Loncey's direction. At the end of his dive, Loncey came to his feet and twisted to face his assailant. Seeing the man approaching with a raised tomahawk, the boy acted without any conscious thought. Instinct fostered by generations of knife-fighting men caused him to whip back his arm and swing it forward, the knife leaving his hand as it had so many times in practice.

Flying steel and charging man converged. An instant too late Raider realized what had happened. He felt the knife's point prick his throat, then its blade sliced home. No child's toy, but a razor-sharp and deadly efficient weapon, the knife sank in at an angle which cut the windpipe and severed both jugular vein and carotid artery. Dying on his feet, Raider still made another attempt to drive his tomahawk into the boy.

Loncey flung himself aside, avoiding the downward swing of the tomahawk, and sprang to catch up his rifle. Even as he pivoted around, the rifle's barrel in Raider's direction, he saw the man let the tomahawk drop, claw weakly up to where the knife's hilt rose from blood-spurting flesh and crash forward to the floor.

12

Sam Ysabel's Decision

Still unaware of his attacker's identity, Loncey stood for a moment and looked down. Violent death was no stranger to him, and the darkness of the tepee prevented the full horror of his act from meeting his eyes. Varied emotions ran through the youngster, but panic was not one of them. He could still think and knew that he must act. While the raider might be a lone warrior seeking loot, he could also be one of a number taking advantage of the Victory Dance to plunder the empty tepees.

Springing across the tepee, Loncey thrust through the axe-slashed door and into the open. He raised his rifle and fired a shot into the air, then threw back his head, letting out a shout in a voice cracked with excitement and emotion.

"An attack!" he yelled. "An attack!"

While a Comanche boy might not be above playing practical jokes on the village, he knew better than to raise a false alarm of that kind. The story of the boy who cried "Wolf"

COMANCHE   131

did not belong exclusively to the white man and a version of it was early drummed into the *Nemenuh* children, to be taken to heart. So, on hearing the shot and Loncey's yell, women fled to safety and the men dashed in the direction from which the alarm had been given.

Among the first to arrive were Ysabel and Long Walker. They had recognized Loncey's voice, which lent speed to their movements.

"What is it, boy?" Ysabel barked.

"A man," Loncey replied, pointing to the tepee. "Inside!"

Without waiting to hear more, Ysabel leapt to the tepee and went through its door. He moved fast, his big Walker Colt held ready for use. Followed by Long Walker, he crossed the floor and halted by the huddled body. Hooking his toe under the body's shoulder, Ysabel rolled it onto its back. In the faint, flickering light thrown by the big fire through the open door, he recognized the shape at his feet.

"Now what the hell?" Ysabel growled.

"It's one of the Antelope braves," Long Walker stated unnecessarily, looking down and sheathing his bowie knife.

"Raider, the dead man's brother," Ysabel confirmed. "But what's he doing in my tepee?"

"That we will learn!" promised Long Walker grimly. "Is Burnt Grass outside?"

One of the men by the door repeated his chief's words and the leader of Fire Dancer's escort entered the tepee. Before Burnt Grass could speak, Long Walker pointed down to the body.

"Raider!" gasped the *Kweharehnuh,* his voice showing baffled amazement and such surprise that the watching men doubted if he could be acting. "What has happened?"

"We do not know, yet," replied Long Walker. "What do you say, Ysabel?"

"Let's have Loncey in and hear his story," suggested Ysabel, "that being his knife in the feller's throat."

During one of his trading trips, Ysabel had picked up a small lantern and fuel oil for it. While Long Walker went to fetch Loncey, Ysabel produced and lit the lamp, using the extra illumination to make a search of the tepee. From what he could see, nothing had been touched or disturbed. That proved little, except that if the dead man planned to steal, he was interrupted before beginning.

Showing no hesitation or concern at being in the tepee with the man he killed, Loncey came through the door. His eyes went first to his father, then in Burnt Grass's direction and he could guess at why he had been called inside.

"Tell it, boy," Ysabel ordered.

"I think your companion should be here to hear, Burnt Grass," Long Walker suggested and the Antelope leader called in his last remaining brave.

Quietly and soberly Loncey began to tell what had happened, starting with his noticing the horse's warning behavior. He went through each part of the incident in order, trying to omit nothing, for he could guess at the gravity of the situation. Not that speaking calmly and plainly came easy, with his father, grandfather and the two *Kweharehnuh* standing in a loose half-circle and studying his face all the time. Then for the first time his eyes strayed to the body and he recognized it as one of the Antelope braves. It seemed that his original guess as to the reason for being called into the tepee was wrong. He had not been brought in to tell of his first coup to the visiting braves, but to explain how he came to kill one of their party.

"I didn't know it was him!" the boy gasped, shocked at discovering he had killed a member of the Comanche Nation and a visitor to their camp. "But all I've told you is true."

"Say the oath, boy!" commanded Long Walker sternly.

Drawing himself erect and setting his face in grim lines, Loncey repeated the words he had learned and heard so often when warriors attested to the truth of their statements.

"Earth, Father. You saw me do it. Sun, Mother. You saw me do it. Do not let me live another season if I speak with a forked tongue."

Burnt Grass nodded gravely as the boy finished the sacred oath. No member of the *Pehnane,* even one so young, ever spoke those words unless telling the truth; they believed implicitly that death would follow should they lie while under the oath's bond of truth.

"It would seem that the boy had no other choice but strike," Hawk Circling commented, examining the gash caused by Raider's tomahawk in the door flap and comparing it with Loncey's height.

There had been little margin for error and the boy must have moved with exceptional speed to avoid the blow of a man like Raider, noted for his skilled use of the fighting axe. Looking across the tepee, Hawk Circling noted that Raider's favorite weapon lay at the right side of the body. Turning his eyes back to Burnt Grass, he gave a satisfied nod.

"We know your son speaks the truth, Ysabel," Burnt Grass declared.

"My thanks," the white man answered formally. "What I want to know is, why did that one come to my tepee and try to kill Loncey."

"A man in grief does strange things," Long Walker pointed out.

"His brother spoke your name in death, Ysabel," Hawk Circling pointed out. "Perhaps he thought that the dying one blamed you for killing him."

"Why?" growled Ysabel. "I'd not spoken a dozen words to either of them, or done more than share food that morning with them. Why'd I want either of them dead?"

"Who knows?" said Hawk Circling vaguely.

"That's an answer I don't reckon helps much," Ysabel answered.

"Hawk Circling and I don't believe such things of you," Burnt Grass assured him and the other *Kweharehnuh* nodded agreement. "But that one—well, he did not think much. If he decided something, he would act, right or wrong."

"He was a brave warrior, though stupid," admitted Hawk Circling.

"Did he say anything to either of you about thinking I poisoned his brother?"

"We never saw him after he left us with his brother in the tepee," replied Burnt Grass. "Even if he believed it, what has happened shows that he was wrong."

"His medicine must have been bad for him to die at the hands of a boy," agreed the other Antelope brave.

Although the Comanche did not go for anything as formal as trial by combat, they firmly believed in the guiding hand of *Ka-Dih* favoring the one in the right of a dispute. That a name warrior of Raider's caliber not only failed to kill, but fell to a boy's knife, meant *Ka-Dih* knew he acted wrongly. The fact gave the *Kweharehnuh* final, definite proof that Raider's suspicions had no basis of truth.

"We do not blame your son for acting as he did, Ysabel," Burnt Grass stated. "He would make a poor braveheart if he did not defend his tepee."

"He will be a name warrior in his time," Hawk Circling went on.

Having seen his son proven innocent of any offense—defending one's tepee, even at the cost of the intruder's life, being regarded as a virtue—Ysabel turned to the boy.

"Go sleep in Loud Voice's tepee for the night, son," he ordered.

Obediently the youngster turned and walked from the tepee. With Loncey out of the way, Ysabel continued to try to find a solution to the mystery. He recalled a point which had been puzzling him ever since meeting the *Kweharehnuh* party.

"Why did Fire Dancer decide to come back to the *Pehnane*?" he asked.

"She told us that she made medicine and dreamed that she must come back to her people to find happiness, having seen much sorrow with losing four husbands."

Except for one fact, the explanation might have satisfied Ysabel. All too well he knew the store set by the Comanches in their medicine-inspired dreams. As he looked at Raider's

body, Ysabel remembered the killing of Bitter Root so many
years back. Of all the dead man's wives, only Fire Dancer
showed real grief. Maybe the woman returned to seek revenge on her first husband's killer. An unlikely happening
for a Comanche woman; but Fire Dancer had been born a
Mexican and the Latin races possessed a capacity for retaining hatreds and seeking vengeance.

However, Ysabel decided to keep his thoughts and suspicions to himself. If the woman had planned to kill him, she
took a mighty roundabout way of doing it. Should she be
after his scalp to avenge Bitter Root, Ysabel figured he stood
a better chance of stopping her while she believed he was in
ignorance of her intentions. And in the event of her being
innocent, with only coincidence to connect her to the braves'
deaths, Ysabel did not wish to spoil her chances of making a
new life among the *Pehnane*.

"Did she ask for the brothers to come along?" he asked.

"No. She had the camp cried asking for men to guide her
here and we said we would come. Life had been slow in our
village for many days."

"Raider's *pairaivo* has an evil tongue, he came to get away
from her," Hawk Circling supplemented to his leader's re-
ply.

"Aiee!" said Burnt Grass. "This is a bad medicine trip for
me. On no more than a visit I lose two men."

"I think this is a bad place, Ysabel," Long Walker put in.
"We will leave tomorrow."

"It'd be as well," Ysabel agreed.

"Hawk Circling and I will ride back to our people," Burnt
Grass announced. "Have no fears, Ysabel, we will see that
no blame is put upon your son."

"Again you have my thanks, *amigo*," Ysabel replied.
"Now let's see to this body. There is much to do before we
break camp tomorrow."

Even the leader of the successful raiding party admitted
the wisdom of moving the camp when Long Walker spoke
with him. Two such mysterious deaths boded little good for

anyone foolish enough to stay in such an area. So an old man rode through the village, crying the news of the impending move and telling everybody by what time they must be ready if they wanted to travel with the main body.

Next day, working with the speed of long practice, the people packed their belongings and dismantled the tepees. Despite the hurried nature of the departure, and the fact that few of the village's inhabitants slept much the previous night, everything went smoothly. Two hours after sunup, the first families moved out on the heels of the horse herds and following the line taken by the warriors of the advance guard.

Instead of riding in his usual place up at the front of the column, Ysabel waited until he saw Raccoon Talker and then swung his grulla alongside her mount.

"What do you make of the Antelope's death, *pia*?" he asked, using the term "mother" as one of respect due to the medicine woman's wisdom and position in life.

"The young one was poisoned," she replied calmly.

"How?"

"That I do not know," Raccoon Talker admitted. "At first I thought that he had eaten the Deadly Amanita mushroom, for that is how one who eats it acts when the poison begins to work. But what grown man would eat that?"

"None, if he knew he was getting it," Ysabel replied.

"Nor could it have been the bad mushroom, for if he ate it early in the morning, he would be dead soon after sundown."

"Could have got it at the dance."

"Then he would not have felt its pains until early this morning. He was not sick, was he?"

Sometimes a Comanche suffering from an incurable disease, or severe illness, would deliberately kill himself rather than become a burden on his people. However Ysabel doubted if that could be the reason for José's death.

"He sure acted lively enough at the dance," he said. "And

he wouldn't've left his own country on a long trip if he'd been that ill."

"I suppose not," the woman said.

"Do you know of any other poisons that he might have eaten?"

"There are a few, but I don't know why he would take them."

"How about if he didn't know he was being given them?"

"There are ways known to witch women," admitted Raccoon Talker. "I have heard of them, but must not speak."

Like her white counterpart, the medicine woman learned many secrets but must not divulge them out of her own circle. Ysabel did not press the matter, for he knew doing so would be a futile waste of time and also offend the woman. Years among the *Pehnane* had given him considerable respect for Raccoon Talker's ability. He knew that he had started to interest her in the affair, or increased her interest, and that she might possibly be able to find the answers which so puzzled them both.

"Perhaps we will never know what happened," he said. "I'd better go and see where we're making camp again."

While swinging away from the line of pack and baggage animals, Ysabel saw War Club riding in his direction after checking on the last village site to make sure nothing of importance had been left behind.

"I'm not sorry to see the back of that place," the *Pehnane* said, drawing alongside Ysabel. "Two men and four dogs died there."

"Four dogs?" repeated the big white man.

"We found them among the bushes."

"I reckon I'd best go back and take a look."

War Club watched Ysabel riding back toward the deserted campsite and scratched his head. No matter how much time he spent in Ysabel's company, he doubted if he would ever understand white men. There did not strike War Club as being anything in the sight of four dead dogs to make the other ride back in order to view their bodies.

Finding the first of the dogs, Ysabel studied its body and
noticed that it showed the same type of contortion as José at
the moment of death. So did all the others, pointing to an
obvious conclusion that all died as a result of the same poison.

Although unsure of·what he sought, Ysabel gave the site
of the village a long search. He found nothing to help him
solve the mystery, for the starving dogs had devoured every
shred of the *awyaw: t* José tossed into his tepee. At last,
puzzled as much as ever, he mounted the grulla and followed the tracks of the traveling band.

Fire Dancer had watched Ysabel talking with Raccoon
Talker, then speak to War Club and ride back toward the
village. Anxiety welled in the Mexican woman and she wondered if she had made some mistake which might lead to her
discovery as the one behind José's and Raider's death. Having received training in their line, Fire Dancer knew something of the powers of a Comanche medicine woman. Once
her interest or suspicions were aroused, Raccoon Talker
possessed sufficient knowledge to be able to ask inconvenient
questions. Fire Dancer knew that she carried enough evidence in her packs to prove her guilt and justice would come
swiftly should the incriminating item be found. Rather than
take a chance, she decided to dispose of the evidence as soon
as possible.

The chance to do so did not come while on the march.
However, the deaths at the old site did not call for a lengthy
journey and, after following the banks of the stream on
which they camped for about two miles upriver, Long
Walker gave the order to halt and settle down.

Without wasting time, the women started to work on
reerecting their homes. Setting up a tepee called for the combined efforts of at least three women, so those like Fire
Dancer, who had no family, had to wait until help came.
After assisting with the erection of their homes, a trio of
naivis came to lend the visitor a hand to raise her tepee.
With the girls' help Fire Dancer soon had everything set up

and her property installed. After thanking the girls for their
help, she watched them head for their homes. Then she
turned to make a start at destroying the evidence to connect
her with the events of the previous night.

Taking up the medicine bag, she carried it from the tepee
and walked slowly through the village. Everybody had
enough work on their hands, so that little or no notice was
taken of the woman. Even the few who saw Fire Dancer
passing paid no attention to her and, if they gave the matter
any thought at all, decided that she must be going to make
medicine away from the village's noise and confusion.

Unfortunately she caught the eye of the one man she
ought to have avoided. Returning from his search of the old
village site, Ysabel saw Fire Dancer leaving at the other side
of the new location. Normally he would have thought nothing of it, but his findings at the old site gave him a lively
interest in the woman's actions.

Leaving his grulla stallion in the care of Long Walker's
pairaivo, he started to follow the woman on foot. While passing through the bushes which bordered the stream, Fire
Dancer kept a watch on her back trail. She saw nothing of
Ysabel, for he could keep out of sight when he wished, as
proved during Loncey's sheep hunt. After walking for almost half a mile Fire Dancer found what she wanted. At
that point the stream rushed through a narrow, deep gorge,
its white-foamed water tearing over and around jagged
rocks. Halting, she looked around and when sure that nobody observed her, opened the medicine bag. Taking out an
awyaw: t of pemmican, she tossed it into the center of the
raging current. With an expression of relief, she closed the
bag and retraced her steps to the village. Although she did
not know it, she passed within a few feet of the well-hidden,
thoughtful Ysabel.

Rising silently from his place of concealment, Ysabel
rubbed a hand across his jaw. While a woman almost invariably carried at least one *awyaw: t* of pemmican among her
property, its storage place was never in the sacred confines

of a medicine bag. The fact made the disposal of the *aw-yaw: t* suspicious, not seeing her throw it into the river. Any woman who found pemmican to be inedible would get rid of it in such a manner if possible, so as to prevent the tainted food falling into the hands of the village's children.

Despite his lack of formal education, Ysabel could think and form conclusions from what he saw. The destruction of the *awyaw: t,* combined with the place in which Fire Dancer carried it and the incidents of the previous night, gave him an insight as to why two men died. Everything began to fall into place; Fire Dancer clearly sought revenge and used José as an innocent dupe to deliver poisoned pemmican to her proposed victim. Only she failed to take into account the young brave's healthy appetite and taste for pemmican. From that Ysabel could see the rest of the affair. Failing with the poisoned pemmican, Fire Dancer played on Raider's grief and sent him to wait in the tepee. Only it had been Loncey who entered, not Ysabel.

Although he knew about the attempts on his life, Ysabel realized that he could prove nothing. If he had known what the medicine bag held, he might have been able to prevent the destruction of the poison-loaded pemmican. After that, it would be for the elders of the tribe to give justice. Now it was only his theories against her word and he knew that the elders would tend to listen more to a medicine woman than a brave.

Ysabel shrugged his broad shoulders and walked back toward the village. Coming from the feuding Kentucky hill country, he could understand Fire Dancer's motives. Against a man the remedy would be simple, but not when dealing with a woman. He decided that he would keep a very careful eye on Fire Dancer in the future and also that in the future it might be best if he took Loncey along whenever he was to be away from the village for any length of time.

13

The Earning of a Man-Name

Life took on a new and fascinating aspect for Loncey after the killing of Raider. No condemnation came his way and all his young companions looked upon him with open admiration. Loncey had achieved the ultimate aim of every well-raised Comanche boy, to kill an enemy in a fair fight. During the few days between the killing and leaving the village on his first smuggling trip, Loncey began to hear himself called by a different name.

Although a Comanche might be given one name at birth, he did not always keep it throughout his life. A brave deed, a special talent, even a mishap or piece of foolishness, could give him a new name. When becoming *tuivitsi* most young *Nemenuh* sought for a change of name, regarding it as a sign of manhood.

Having noticed the affinity Loncey showed for handling the knife, it took only his use of that weapon to kill an enemy for people to know what his man-name should be. At first only his companions spoke the man-name openly, older heads being content to wait and see if he lived up to the title. To the boys of his particular band, Loncey became *Cuchillo,* which was Spanish for knife.

For the first time upon the trip, Loncey saw how the white men lived and wondered how they managed to change village sites when dwelling in such huge wooden tepees. At first he felt shy, nervous almost, but his adaptable nature soon drove such alien feelings from him. At that time in Texas, the term "squaw man" had not come to be derogatory. Nobody held Ysabel's marriage against him, nor Loncey's Indian blood. Such boys as he met in the small Texas towns soon came to admire him, especially when he demonstrated his Indian-trained skills.

Not that Loncey spent much time in the small towns. After selling a consignment of hides and skins, Ysabel pushed on to Jack County. Four Mexican prisoners helped him in his trading. Captured as boys, they no longer wished to return to the life of a peon below the border and gave willing assistance. In Jack County the party picked up supplies, including the home-brewed whiskey for which the area became famous, and other goods much sought after in Mexico.

Then began the boy's long, rewarding association with the Mexican people. He already spoke some Spanish, most Comanches did, and soon became fluent in accent or dialect as needed. During the three months the boy spent in Mexico, he made many friends and became an especial favorite of Don Francisco Almonte. While visiting the Don's hacienda, Loncey was encouraged to make the place his home. From Almonte he received added instruction in the art of using a knife and learned all Casa Almonte's secrets. Loncey had cause to be thankful for the Don's instruction in the finer points of knife fighting and would one day repay his debt to the Mexican.*

* Told in *The Peacemakers.*

Returning to the *Pehnane* country, Loncey slipped once more into the flow of village life. In a way he felt cheated, for the entire trip had been profitable and uneventful, producing no adventure nor chance to distinguish himself.

Watched over by Ysabel and Long Walker, to whom the white man confided his suspicions, Fire Dancer failed to make any further attempts at revenge. When the war lodges gathered for the prewinter buffalo-hunting season, she transferred her tepee to the Owl lodge and started to act as medicine woman. On the few occasions that they met, Loncey and No Father formed a mutual dislike. However, at that time No Father was under a disadvantage, for he could not show a single exploit to come close to the deeds by which Loncey won his fame.

For almost three more years Loncey ranged the Rio Grande with his father, or traveled among the *Pehnane.* During that time he came to know the big river intimately, learning its secret fords and dangerous areas. Among the other white men involved in the smuggling, Loncey started by being called Sam Ysabel's kid and in time that became shortened to the name by which he would gain considerable fame, the Ysabel Kid. The Mexicans of the border learned to know him and named him *Cabrito,* Spanish for a young goat, but spoke the word with respect as they saw his way when crossed. When first addressed as *Cabrito,* Loncey took exception to the name. Fortunately for the man who said it, the boy was prevented from making his objections too strenuously, for Loncey fought like a Comanche, to the death.

They were hard, dangerous years ideally suited to molding Loncey into the deadly efficient fighting man he became. Everything he had learned among the *Pehnane* came in useful. Not every trip went smoothly. Sometimes there would be long chases to avoid capture by revenue-enforcing soldiers, or outlaws wanting to snatch the smuggled goods by force. Three times in brushes with the latter, Loncey had to kill a man, but using his rifle, not the knife. In the end Mexican *bandidos* and white outlaws learned it did not pay

to attempt robbery against the Ysabel outfit. Ambushes
failed, due to the Comanche-trained alertness of the boy
called the Ysabel Kid; and any outfit which came within
long-rifle range soon wished it had not, for Loncey fulfilled
his earlier promise as a marksman.

In the early afternoon about a week after his fourteenth
birthday, Loncey rode at his father's side through wooded
country not far from the Rio Grande. Following their usual
procedure, they traveled about a hundred yards ahead of
their Mexican helpers and well-laden packhorses. Seeing a
couple of riders approaching, Ysabel made a signal which
caused the Mexicans to swing off the trail beyond the approaching duo's range of vision and take cover.

"Lawmen!" Loncey grunted, fingers coiled around his
Mississippi rifle ready to use it. "Do we fight?"

"Not agin that pair, boy," Ysabel answered. "It's Hondo
Fog and Branston Blaze from over Rio Hondo way."

While Loncey knew the names, he had not yet met the
two men in question. One area all smugglers steered well
clear of was Rio Hondo County. Owned and controlled by
three fighting Texas families, with clear title granted to them
for services rendered to the state, Rio Hondo County could
claim the most efficient law-enforcement west of the Mississippi. Brave, skilled with their weapons, incorruptible, Sheriff Hondo Fog and his deputy, Branston Blaze, kept the
peace. Nobody with a smidgen of good Texas sense tangled
with them.

"Howdy Hondo, Branston," greeted Ysabel, having continued riding toward the two men. "You're a fair piece from
home."

"Could say the same about you, Sam," replied the sheriff.
"This your boy?"

"Yep. Say howdy to the sheriff, boy."

Loncey gave a grunt which could have meant anything.
Then he found himself forming a liking for the big, power-
ful-looking, blond sheriff. Dressed in a wide-brimmed black
hat, buckskin jacket, pants tucked into riding boots, with a

Dragoon Colt holstered at his right side and a Colt revolving rifle across his saddle, Hondo Fog struck Loncey as being very much a man. Branston Blaze too, tall, red-haired, dressed and armed in the same manner as the sheriff, seemed more pleasant and amiable than most peace officers the boy had met.

"What brings you out this way, Hondo?" Ysabel inquired after the boy gave a greeting.

"Montego," the sheriff answered.

"Figured somebody'd get around to looking for him one of these days," grunted Ysabel, knowing the name to be that of a notorious *Comanchero* and *bandido.* "What's he done this time?"

"Called on the Hobills."

Something in Hondo Fog's quiet tones brought Ysabel's eyes to the sheriff's face. "Bad?" asked Ysabel.

"Killed Ma, Pa, and the three boys."

"How about lil Mary-Sue?"

"They killed her," Blaze put in, not hiding his emotion as well as the sheriff. "After—"

"He's a bad *hombre,*" said Ysabel quietly. "Always has been. And you pair aim to go in there to tangle with him and all his bunch?"

"There's a company of U.S. Mounted Rifles following us," Hondo explained. "The Yankees've decided to shake the bulldroppings from their socks and call time on skunks like Montego."

"Reckon you can find him for 'em, Hondo?"

"I *thought* we could. They split up into small bunches after hitting at the Hobill place. Bran and I took after one bunch, lost their trail back that way a piece and hoped to find it again down here."

"They've not come this way, that's for sure," Ysabel stated. "Can them Yankee soldier boys find *you*?"

"Ole Devil sent Kiowa along with us," Hondo answered.

Knowing the man named was half Indian, Ysabel admit-

ted he might be able to lead the soldiers to the sheriff. "Go
find that trail for the sheriff, boy," he said.

Loncey had sat silent, but his mind turned over everything he heard. While he did not care for the idea of helping
the law, he felt that for once he might stretch a point. Without having it explained, Loncey could guess what had happened to the Hobill family. He knew them, having visited
their small ranch on more than one occasion and always
been made welcome. So, realizing what the cryptic words
about the Hobills' fate meant, he paused only a moment
before moving to obey his father's command.

"Where'd you lose their tracks?" he asked before moving.

"We'll take you there," Hondo answered.

"My girth's come loose," Ysabel remarked casually.
"Ride on, I'll fix it."

"Sure," agreed the sheriff. "Tell your boys to swing west
and stay clear of the trails, there're more than one patrol
out."

"Never could stand a smart-aleck lawman," grinned
Ysabel and rode directly to his concealed men without trou-
bling to make a pretense at tightening a perfectly satisfactory girth.

On being taken to the point at which the sheriff realized
the trail had been lost, Loncey started to circle around.
Working in an ever increasing circumference, he at last
picked up the sign of passing horses. No mean hand at read-
ing sign himself, Hondo Fog decided that he rated low on
the scale when compared with that tall, slim, baby-faced
boy. Admiration showed on the sheriff's face as he watched
the Kid track for the first time. Little did either of them
know that in the future Hondo would be able to call upon
the Kid's services regularly.

For three miles the boy followed sign which only his father could read most of the time. It said much for Hondo
Fog's trust in Ysabel that he accepted the boy's lead even
when unable to see any reason for going in that particular
direction. However, after the second mile Hondo received

proof of the boy's accuracy when the track grew more plain due to another segment of the gang joining the one they followed. Two more groups joined in soon after and the sign showed more plainly.

Drawing his horse to a halt, Loncey looked around him with some interest. "Obregon's place is just over the rim there, *'ap.*"

"You're right, boy," Ysabel answered. "They'll likely be inside."

While Hondo Fog had heard of Obregon's cantina, he could not have said for sure whether it lay near or far from their current position. However, he accepted the boy's word and followed as Loncey dropped from the horse and advanced on foot up the slope ahead of them. For a white man, and peace officer to boot, Hondo showed considerable knowledge of certain basic matters Loncey believed only a Comanche appreciated. Coming up on foot, the sheriff moved silently and kept well below the head of the rim as he and the boy peeped over.

From what met Hondo's eyes, he judged that the boy led him well. Out in the floor of the valley lay Obregon's cantina; a pair of really fine horses stood tied to its hitching rail. In the adobe-walled corral, some twenty good mounts moved restlessly.

"The whole bunch's there," Hondo breathed, watching a tall, well-dressed and heavily armed Mexican walk from the cantina to the horses at the hitching rail.

"That's Montego," Loncey informed the sheriff.

"It figures, boy. Let's go talk to your pappy."

Hondo did not need discussion to see the difficulty in capturing Montego's band. Taking the cantina would create no serious problem. A notorious hideout for the worst kind of border thieves, it could be reduced from the rim by the lightweight 12-pounder howitzer carried sectionally on muleback with the soldiers. That would be the only way in which the cantina could be taken without considerable risk and loss of life, for it was built in the center of the valley and insufficient

cover prevented any chance of a large body of men moving
in close. Even using the howitzer would not be of much
more use. At the first shot, Montego's bunch would be running for their horses. The Rio Grande glinted about a half
mile away, offering a safe refuge to the Mexican nationals
once they crossed it.

"They've sure picked a swell place," Hondo concluded,
after explaining the situation to the other two men.

"We couldn't catch up to them before they'd be mounted
and over the border," Branston Blaze complained bitterly.

"Which same's why Obregon's place is so popular,"
Ysabel drawled. "He's got a lousy cook."

"There has to be a way—" Hondo growled.

"You could nail them afore they hit the river was they
afoot," said Ysabel.

"Only they won't be," the sheriff pointed out. "That corral's gate faces the cantina. Even if we put down the guard
they'll have on it and let the horses out, Montego's bunch
would start running for the border."

"If they knew the hosses had gone, they would," Ysabel
agreed, looking to where Loncey now stood listening.
"How'd you like to try your hand at raiding, boy?"

"Would I just, *'ap!*" enthused the boy.

The old Comanche pursuit of raiding meant appropriat-
ing horses, any other loot gathered being merely a secondary
consideration. Every properly constituted *Pehnane* boy lived
for the day when he could make his first essay into the noble
art. Having studied the corral, Loncey could foresee no
great difficulty. In fact he regarded the adobe walls as a
positive asset rather than a danger.

"How soon do you reckon those blue bellies'll be here,
Hondo?" Ysabel asked.

"Could likely bring them in by dawn, if Branston goes
and guides them here," the sheriff replied. "Kiowa can't
track in the dark."

"When they get here, can you hold them back until everything's set, happen they come afore we're through with the hosses?"

"I reckon I can," grinned Hondo. "Ole Devil had a few words with their commander before we left the OD Connected."

Which meant the officer would be more amenable to suggestions than most of his kind when dealing with civilians. At that time, as in later life even after being crippled trying to ride an unbroken horse,* Ole Devil Hardin packed considerable weight in Texas affairs. No army captain with an eye on his future would ignore the suggestions of a man in Ole Devil's favor.

"Then we'll give her a whirl," Ysabel drawled.

"How do you plan to handle it?" Hondo asked, after Blaze rode off to collect the soldiers.

"Nemenuh fashion," Ysabel replied and patted the Comanche hair rope on his grulla's saddle.

Moving silently through the darkness, Loncey, Ysabel and the sheriff made their way to the rear of the corral. Already one guard stood by the gate and, even as the trio approached, a second man left the cantina.

"What now?" Ysabel breathed as the second man walked toward the guard.

"We'll have to take them both," Hondo answered in no louder tone. "I'll go to the right, you have the one on the left."

"Let's wait and see if the one being relieved goes in first," suggested Ysabel.

Although they waited, the hope was not fulfilled. Instead of going to the cantina, as any decent guard should when relieved, the first man stayed talking to his relief.

"We'll have to take them," Hondo said.

"Looks that way," Ysabel answered and laid down the rope he carried.

Much as he would have liked to go along, Loncey realized

---

* Told in *The Fastest Gun in Texas.*

he could not waste time in arguing the matter. Not having been raised in the Comanche tradition, Hondo regarded fourteen as being just a mite young for the risky business of silencing horse guards, especially as the boy was armed only with a knife and could not club a man insensible with that.

Leaving Loncey, the men moved off around the walls of the corral. Ysabel made no sound as he passed along the side and turned to the front. Ahead of him, the two guards stood talking in low tones. Clearly they expected no trouble, for they showed none of their usual alertness and their voices carried to him.

"How that small one screamed," the man with his back to Ysabel was saying. "Hah! How I enjoyed it."

"So you should have," his companion replied. "You were the last to have her."

With those words, a man forfeited his right to stay alive. Up until that moment Ysabel intended to use the butt of his big Walker Colt to silence the guard. On hearing that one of the men who raped Mary-Sue Hobill stood before him, he substituted the bowie knife for his gun.

Suddenly Hondo Fog loomed behind the second man, coming as silently as Ysabel from the opposite direction. Up swung the sheriff's arm and lashed toward the man's head. Even as the guard before Ysabel realized the danger, a big hand closed over his mouth from behind and dragged him back onto the point of the bowie knife. Savagely Ysabel rammed home the knife into the guard's kidneys. His hand stifled any outcry, and death came swiftly. After a brief, convulsive jerking, the guard went limp and Ysabel let a lifeless body fall to the ground.

"Did you have to kill him?" demanded the sheriff as Ysabel wiped the knife's blade clean on the dead man's clothing.

"I reckon Mary-Sue Hobill'd say I did," Ysabel answered. "Hawgtie you'rn, I'll prop mine up by the gate so that anybody looking from the cantina'll think they still have a guard out."

Being an advocate for simple justice, Hondo raised no more objections. He had heard the conversation between the guards and knew why Ysabel struck to kill. Taking out the pigging thongs brought for the purpose, he secured the unconscious man at his feet and gagged him with his own bandana. By the time Hondo finished, Ysabel had propped up the body by the gate.

Dragging the prisoner between them, the two men returned to where Loncey stood. Ysabel did not need to speak to his son. As Hondo went to keep watch on the cantina from the corner of the corral, Loncey bounded up, caught hold of the top of the wall and pulled himself over. Taking up his rope, Ysabel tossed one end over to his son. However, Loncey left the rope hanging for a moment. Swiftly he passed among the resting horses, calming down any which showed signs of restlessness, until he found the dominant animal. Being herd creatures, horses always accepted one of their number as leader and followed its lead. If the scheme was to succeed, Loncey must pick out that horse from among the others. All the experience gained during his training years went into the search and at last Loncey made his decision. Catching hold of the remuda leader's mane, he led the horse to where the rope hung.

With everything ready at his side, Loncey gripped the rope and shook it gently. Then he drew down on his end, whipping the hard rope over the top of the wall. At the other side, Ysabel waited until his son's pull ended, then drew back on his end.

Back and forward, back and forward went the rope, its rough exterior acting as a saw and biting into the adobe blocks of the wall. It required much continuous effort, but man and boy worked on without stopping until they had cut down almost to the ground. Pulling free their rope, they moved it about three feet to the left of the first cut and repeated the process.

Time dragged by. At the cantina light after light went out, but Hondo knew at least one guard would be awake in the building. Apparently nobody missed the first corral sentry, although that could be because Montego meant to keep two men watching the vital horses.

On reaching ground level with the second cut, Ysabel and Loncey took a rest but did not remove the rope. Instead they started to draw the strands along parallel to the ground in the direction of the right-hand incision.

"Easy, boy!" Ysabel hissed at last.

Reaching up, Ysabel gripped the top of the wall and pulled at it. For a moment nothing happened, then the cutaway segment tilted outward and Ysabel lowered it to the ground.

"Here, *'ap!*" Loncey said, voice throbbing with excitement but only a whisper.

Everything depended on how well the boy judged the horses. Ysabel caught the mane of the animal Loncey selected and led it through the gap. Instantly the boy started the next animal moving, but left it to quiet a third horse which began to show signs of becoming restless. Such was the skill Loncey had developed that he kept the remuda quiet while leading out horse after horse. Finding their companions departing, the remaining horses showed no reluctance at being woken from sleep and led out to where Ysabel, mounted on their leader, waited. At last every horse had been collected and Ysabel started walking the leader slowly away, with the rest following behind.

14
An Old Feud Revived

"Where's Loncey?" asked Hondo as he and Ysabel moved the horses up the slope of the valley.

For the first time Ysabel realized that his son was not accompanying them. Twisting around, he looked back to the corral and from there in the direction of the cantina. Suddenly he knew the answer to the sheriff's question.

"The damned young fool!" Ysabel growled. "He's gone after those other two horses that're out front."

"What're we going to do?" Hondo inquired.

"Keep going," replied Ysabel. "Happen the boy can't fend for himself by now, Long Walker and me raised him all wrong."

With that Ysabel continued moving up the slope and Hondo followed. Already the deep blackness which comes just before dawn breaks had descended. If they were to succeed, the men must have the horses over the rim before Montego's gang stirred in the cantina. On topping the slope, both men looked back, but beyond the black loom of the cantina's bulk and corral walls could discern nothing of what went on down below.

Two ideas motivated Loncey's decision to collect the pair of fine horses from before the cantina. First he wished to distinguish himself by an act of bravery as had always been taught to him. Secondly he knew that Hondo meant to have the pair shot when the attack started, so as to prevent the men in the cantina using them.

Closing the gap between the corral and the cantina, Loncey moved in complete silence and his buckskin clothing merged with the blackness around him. Although no lights showed from the cantina, he did not become careless. So he heard the squeak of the front door and instantly sank to the ground in a crouch, right hand sliding the knife from its sheath.

A man walked from the cantina, sombrero on head and serape draped around him. Muttering to himself, he started to cross the open ground in the direction of the corral. Loncey knew what he must do. If the man found the denuded corral, he would raise the alarm and spoil all the good work of the night. Swiftly the boy thought of his instruction in the business of silencing an enemy. In often-repeated lessons, he had been taught where to use a knife at such a time so as to ensure a quick and silent death. Walking with his head bowed forward, the man prevented any chance of slashing the throat. Nor could Loncey be sure of striking any of the places in the body under the concealment of the serape.

Only one place remained—but it was one of the best for Loncey's purpose, even if only a knife-fighter would think of it.

Nearer came the man, unaware of his danger. Half-asleep, unattentive, he paid the ultimate price for lack of caution. Like a flash Loncey came up from the ground, his knife licking forward. The razor-sharp blade tore open the inside of the man's left thigh, slicing in to sever both the femoral and great saphenous veins. Even as pain drove into the man, numbing his mind, Loncey's left hand caught his uninjured leg at the ankle and hauled it from the ground. Down went the man, his rifle falling from his hand but not exploding. Dropping onto his victim, Loncey forced the sombrero over the man's face and stifled any chance of an outcry during the thirty seconds needed for death to come.

Rising from the body, Loncey looked around him. All remained still; his silencing appeared to have been successful. He walked forward, approaching the two horses and whistling in a low, tuneless manner which tended to sooth any fears they might have. The nearer animal must have caught a smell of blood, for it snorted and moved restlessly. Darting forward, Loncey caught its headstall with his left hand and commenced to quiet it in the manner learned so well during horse-stealing games at the village.

The man who left the cantina had bare feet and made little or no sound. Pausing outside, he glanced toward the horses and saw the dark human shape close by. Unsure of who it might be, but apparently suspecting nothing, he walked forward.

"What's wro—?" he began.

Fast and deadly as a stick-teased rattlesnake, Loncey whirled around. He had heard the man's approach and wasted not a single moment. Before the newcomer realized his mistake, Loncey struck. This one did not wear a hat and the boy knew just what to do. Across and up whipped his right arm, ripping the knife's blade over the man's throat. Deep into flesh sank the steel, slicing the windpipe, vocal cords and veins until almost touching the bone, preventing its receiver from being able to utter any sound. Turning, the man staggered, clutching at the hitching rail with his left hand while trying to draw the revolver from his sash with the right. Death came just as quickly as it had with his companion and he slid to the ground without making a sound.

"*A'he!*" Loncey hissed automatically.

Behind him the horses showed signs of becoming restless. For all that Loncey stepped to the dying man and pulled the gun from his sash, a precaution against a last-minute burst of strength and determination drawing and firing it to waken the still-sleeping cantina. The smooth, hand-fitting curve of a Dragoon Colt's walnut butt and the four-pound, one-ounce weight told Loncey what kind of revolver he held. It seemed that *Ka-Dih* looked in favor on the boy that night, not only permitting him to count coup twice, but also presenting him with the opportunity to obtain a highly prized piece of loot. Already the Colt company had begun to build its reputation and receive just acclaim for the excellence of its products. Among the *Pehnane* no firearm was so highly prized as the heavy, six-shot Colt revolving pistol—as it was known at that time—and, by right of possession, Loncey now owned one.

Sheathing his knife, he thrust the revolver into his belt and went to the horses. With remarkably steady fingers, considering what he had just done, the boy unfastened the reins. He did not mount, but led the animals slowly away from the building. Already disturbed by the smell of blood, the horses showed no objections to moving away from its source. Once clear of the hard-packed earth before the cantina, with springy, sound-deadening grass underfoot, Loncey mounted one of the horses to ride it and led the other up the slope.

"See you got them," Ysabel grunted as his son joined him and the sheriff.

"They're good horses, *'ap*," Loncey replied, giving all the excuses he considered necessary. "The soldiers are coming."

Not for several more seconds could Hondo Fog hear the distant sound of horses moving. He glanced up at the sky, which lightened by the minute. Taking the *bandidos'* mounts had been justified, for the soldiers would not arrive until after it became sufficiently light to prevent any chance of their reaching the cantina unseen. Given even moderate luck now, Branston Blaze would have the men on hand and the attack launched before any of the *bandidos* became aware of the loss of the horses.

"You be needing us anymore, Hondo?" asked Ysabel.

"I don't reckon so," answered the sheriff, knowing his companion did not wish to meet the soldiers.

"How about the hosses?"

"The laborer is worthy of his hire," quoted Hondo. "Take them."

"Now here's a lawman I could get to like," drawled Ysabel.

"You try running contraband through Rio Hondo and you'll quick change your mind on that," grinned Hondo. "And thanks, Sam."

"See you around, Hondo," Ysabel replied. "Let's go, boy."

With the coming of daylight, Ysabel found just how worthwhile his son's private raid had been. The two horses each sported a fancy, silver-concha decorated saddle and bridle, while being animals of considerable value. Studying the horses, Loncey felt content. He knew that he had performed a feat worthy of a *Nemunuh* brave.

Just how worthwhile Loncey did not learn until much later. Even Hondo Fog failed to find out until after the attack on the cantina had been successfully made, for he withdrew to go and meet the soldiers before it was light enough to see the two dead men outside the building.

Although the men arrived and began their advance before the loss of the horses was discovered, an occupant of the cantina saw them and raised the alarm. At first the *bandidos* prepared to make their fight from the bulletproof safety of the building, but a shell from the howitzer changed their minds. Dashing out, they found the corral empty and at that moment Hondo gave the order to launch a charge.

Knowing the cornered-rat courage of the *bandido,* Hondo felt puzzled at the comparatively weak resistance. He found the reason when advancing to secure the men who surrendered. The few who tried to reach the safety of the Rio

Grande on foot were run down by a mounted party under
Branston Blaze. Sprawled before the building, clearly dead
before the attack, lay two bodies.

"It's Montego and his second-in-command," Hondo told
the U.S. Mounted Rifles officer.

"That accounts for why the others didn't fight," replied
the officer. "They had no leader. Your work, sheriff?"

Looking down at Montego, lying with bare feet and fancy
clothing soaked in the blood which poured from the ear-to-
ear gash in the throat, Hondo shook his head.

"Not mine. The Ysabel Kid's."

"Here, brother," said Loncey, standing in the center of a
circle of people and passing the reins of one of the cantina
horses to Loud Voice. Then he turned and looked at Comes
For Food. "And this is for you, *amigo.*"

After rejoining their Mexican helpers, Loncey and Ysabel
pushed on to the *Pehnane* country. They found the village
with no great difficulty, returning in the manner of a triumphant raiding party. Having brought in a fair bunch of
horses, including the two acquired by his own efforts, gained
possession of a Colt revolver and counted coup twice,
Loncey could only be honored by receiving another Give-
Away Dance. For the first time, he was in a position to be
able to supply the majority of the gifts arranged in the center
of the circle and took a warrior's right by ensuring that his
foster brother and best friend received the pick of the loot.

Nobody expected a braveheart to part with such a highly
desirable trophy as the Dragoon Colt, of course. It proved to
be one of the straight-backed trigger-guard type later known
as the First Model, almost in mint condition and not altered
from when it left the factory. A store in the last white man's
town visited before entering the *Pehnane* country supplied
Loncey with a Colt powder flask suitable for the Dragoon
and a .44 caliber bullet mold. While offered paper cartridges,
the boy declined. He preferred to use a round lead ball
backed by forty grains of loose powder. Such was the sim-

plicity of design and operation that Loncey could strip, clean, maintain and load his weapon long before he reached the village, but handling it with accuracy took far more practice.

It seemed that the fates conspired to keep alive Fire Dancer's hatred of the Ysabel family. Only the day before, No Father made his first major hunting kill, a large bull elk, and his mother planned to give a dance to make sure everybody knew of his achievement. Unfortunately a mere hunting trophy could not compare with the horses brought in by Loncey and so Fire Dancer's celebration had to be postponed while the village honored the greater success. Such would have been intolerable to Fire Dancer under any conditions; that a member of the hated Ysabel family caused her son's being forgotten made matters far worse.

After Loncey told of his exploits, with the crowd listening and the braves nodding grim approval, Ysabel walked to his side. Holding out his hand, the big man asked to see the boy's knife. Obediently Loncey handed it over, watching as his father examined it. At last Ysabel gave a grunt and tossed the knife aside.

"That was for a boy to carry," he said, reaching behind his back and producing something hidden beneath his pants waistband. "But this is a man's knife. Take it—*Cuchillo.*"

Only by straining every nerve did Loncey prevent himself from showing the emotion which welled up inside him at what he saw. In his father's hands lay a knife—yet such a knife as the boy only dreamed of owning. It had an ivory hilt curved so as to fit in the palm and never slip, a brass guard to protect the hand from an enemy's cut or stab, and a blade a full eleven and a half inches long, two and a half wide, thick across the back for strength, yet with an edge a barber might desire on his razor, the convex swoop of the edge forming a central point with a two and a half inch concave false edge on the back, the latter so sharpened as to form a continuation of the blade itself.

Loncey did not need to ask what kind of knife his father

presented to him. There might be good copies available, but only the true, genuine James Black bowie knife gave that impression of superlative excellence. Bought some time before, the knife had been stored in buffalo tallow and kept hidden until Long Walker and Ysabel decided the boy to be worthy of owning it. Loncey's actions at the cantina proved him to be ready to take possession of one of the finest fighting knives ever made.

Standing in the light of the fire, Loncey hefted the knife and tried a tentative slash. He felt the knife's superb balance throw its weight behind the blade and knew he held perfection when he mastered its use. A dull rumble rose from the watching crowd, a single word. Yet in the moment the boy was Loncey no more to the *Pehnane*. At last he received formal granting of his man-name. It rolled like distant thunder through the still of the Texas night.

"Cuchillo!"

"Look at him!" hissed Fire Dancer, standing in the darkness at the edge of the crowd and jabbing her son with an elbow. "You are a better warrior than him, yet they give him honor and none to you."

While No Father heartily agreed with his mother's views on his greatness, he grudgingly admitted that nothing he had so far achieved even approached the deeds which brought Loncey acclaim. Of course he could seek to devalue the slim boy by physical means, but had no wish to make the attempt. While No Father wished to achieve the greatness his mother frequently prophesied, he possessed a broad streak of caution and felt disinclined to take unnecessary risks. All too well he knew the other boy's deadly fighting skill and did not aim to tangle with Loncey, *Cuchillo* as he now was, unless sure of holding the advantage.

"I will kill him!" No Father promised.

"So my medicine tells me," his mother assured him.

"Does it tell you when and how?"

"Only that you must watch your chance and take it when it comes."

Which, while not satisfactory, proved to be the only answer No Father received. However, once the idea had been planted in his head, he devoted much thought to how he might find a safe, sure way to bring about the other boy's death.

Further fuel was added to No Father's hate when it became apparent that he could not arouse interest in celebrating his big kill. The time being mid-October, everybody in the village thought only of the forthcoming winter buffalo hunts. At that period of the year, only a major event like Loncey's could distract public interest from what amounted to the *Pehnane*'s harvest time. With the Give-Away Dance ended, preparations for the big hunt began.

During the days which followed, No Father received little or no chance to make a move against Loncey. With so many exploits to his credit, Loncey found himself the hero of the young and adolescent boys. However, a few resented his fame and among them No Father recruited a small band of followers. Try though he might, No Father failed to stir any of his band into chancing an attack on Loncey. So matters rested and the everyday life of the village continued its flow toward the supreme period of the year.

Naturally such a major event could not be jumped into without planning and preparation. While scouts ranged far in search of the choicest herds, men saw to their weapons and women made ready packs, hunting tents, supplies of food to be used while away from the main village. For all the hard work involved, everybody showed the best of spirits, looking forward to plenty of food and the gathering of the necessities of life. Each night the Buffalo Dance fires blazed and an even number of musicians, never an odd, beat out the traditional rhythms for all who wished to join in.

When the scouts returned, a huge council gathered, listened to the reports and gravely debated the findings. At last, when all who wished had spoken their piece, the war chiefs gave a decision on where the hunt would take place and went into details of its organization.

On the appointed day, almost four weeks after the preparations began, the majority of able-bodied men, women and older children left the village. Only a small, well-armed guard remained behind to protect the younger children, old people, tepees and property. With numerous pack animals, the hunters rode out in search of the big herd on which they intended to live until the summer hunts. Even at the temporary camp, the Buffalo Dances continued. These had no religious significance, the coming of the buffalo still being so assured that no medicine was required to find them, but merely served to show everybody's high spirits.

Working swiftly, the men cut poles and erected scaffolds upon which the meat could be hung to dry in the sun and the women put up hunting tents made of a couple of undressed hides draped over a wooden frame in the fashion of a white soldier's pup tent.

When all had been made ready, the hunting began. Several parties had been formed, each under the command of a noted hunter. By common consent Ysabel led his group and took along Loncey, Comes For Food and Loud Voice. Being of the right age, No Father also attended the hunt, working with an Owl lodge party. The boy brought along a Hawken rifle as well as his bow and arrows.

Long experience had taught the Comanche never to use a saddle when hunting buffalo. Such strenuous work put the horses involved under a strain and every extra ounce of weight carried lessened the chances of success. To offer some assistance in riding and using the bow, a rope would be wound loosely about the horse's body just behind its forelegs. With his knees in the coils, the rider stayed on in safety if not comfort. Stripped to their breechclouts, with full quivers on the shoulders, the hunters gathered before dawn and rode out with their leaders. Although Ysabel and Loncey each left his rifle behind, knowing the bow to be superior for their kind of hunting, they retained their gun belts, each with a revolver butt forward in its holster on the right and sheathed bowie knife at the left. Some of the men carried lances instead of bows, but they belonged to the elite of the tribe who used the same weapon in war and scorned to fight from a distance.

The ideal location for a herd was in a narrow valley with numerous ravines splitting from it. In such an area, the hunters formed a semicircle around the grazing animals, mounted but staying downwind and concealed. On their leader's signal, the men charged down on the herd, rapidly forming a complete circle. Properly executed, the surround —as it was called—made the herd bunch and not try to run, and allowed easy killing.

Unfortunately Ysabel's party did not find their herd in such a place, but grazing out on open land which did not allow for the neat surround. So he held his men in a line and they stalked carefully from downwind toward their prey. While the buffalo had a fair sense of smell, being essentially a creature of vast herds made it far less wary than deer, antelope or elk.

Sitting the buffalo-trained horse loaned to him by Long Walker, Loncey watched the herd and restrained his eagerness. For once the individualistic Comanche did not give free rein to their desires, but stayed obedient to orders. A premature rush by a small group might easily scatter the herd and certainly cause it to run. Meat from an animal overheated by a long chase spoiled quickly, so the mass rush which brought a number of the animals down was needed to prevent long chases.

Loncey locked an arrow to his bowstring and felt the horse quiver under him. Much as he enjoyed the prospect, he wished that he owned and had trained the horse. That would be the last, final sign of manhood: to capture, break and train his own horse, turning it into the friend, companion and guard which a warrior's favorite mount must be.

All thoughts of horse training fled abruptly as Ysabel, satisfied that the moment had come, gave the signal to charge. From a slow, cautious walk, the line sprang forward in a wild rush, its flank turning in to form a crescent and try to encircle the herd. Too late the buffalo realized their danger and started to lumber away across the plains.

Riding like the wind, Loncey led the flank riders toward the herd. His attention centered upon a young bull in the prime of condition. Without needing more guidance than a knee-touch in the required direction, the horse ranged itself slightly behind and on the fleeing bull's right side. Drawing back his bow until the arrow's flight brushed his cheek, Loncey aimed at the area between the bull's hip bone and short rib. Only there could he hope to obtain sufficient penetration for his purpose. A buffalo's heart lay low in its chest cavity and an arrow launched from above stood its best chance of reaching the vital organs at that angle.

Wise in the ways of buffalo, the horse started to swing away as the bow twanged and arrow flew. If a charge came from the wounded bull, the horse aimed to be clear of it. Loncey heard a thud and twisted his head to see the bull sliding with buckled legs and head on the ground, to crash onto its side. Even as he whooped his joy, he felt something strike the horse, thought he heard a shot mingled with the thunder and grunting of the fleeing buffalo and scream from the horse.

Only before the sound could register in his mind, he felt the horse falling under him.

15

The White Stallion

Without conscious thought, Loncey realized his danger and reacted to it at top speed. Jerking his knees from the rope, he tossed his left leg over the falling horse's back and thrust himself clear. Years of practice saved him, for he landed on his feet with all the agility of a cat. Even though he did not fall, the boy found himself to still be in serious danger. During the rush, his light weight enabled the horse to carry him ahead of his companions and he had been up with the leaders of the fleeing herd when the accident happened.

Led by a big bull, a considerable section of the herd swung in the boy's direction and came boiling down on him. Fortunately the bull turned ahead of the others, its following merely acting on herd instinct. Down went Loncey's right hand, turning palm out and closing on the Dragoon's butt. While he could not make a real fast draw, he brought out the revolver in a passably swift move. His left hand came across to close on the right and give support, while both thumbs eased back the hammer. From so close that he could not possibly miss, Loncey fired and drove a bullet into the center of the bull's lowered head. Forty grains of black powder gave the old Dragoon revolver a power unequaled in handguns until the coming of high-grade steel and smokeless explosives, so the bullet shattered through the bone of the skull and into the brain beyond. Down went the bull, crumpling forward and sliding along the ground.

Loncey flung himself to one side, avoiding the dead bull, but he was not yet out of danger. More of the herd thundered down, trampling upon the fallen horse in their flight. Yet no buffalo ever went over the body of a fallen companion, so Loncey sprang forward to land on the bull's back and lie there. Shaggy bodies brushed by on either side as the herd split around the dead bull, leaving the boy untouched.

With the danger past, Loncey dropped to the ground and looked around him. The dust churned up by hunters and hunted swirled away and he could see the result of the run. Not until then did any of the others notice his predicament, so busy and engrossed had they been. Whirling his horse, Ysabel galloped toward his son with Loud Voice and Comes For Food hot on his heels.

"What happened, boy?" asked Ysabel.

"I'm not sure, '*ap*," Loncey replied. "But I thought I heard a shot and then the horse fell."

Dropping from his saddle, Ysabel strode to the fallen horse and looked down. In passing the buffalo had hooked the horse with their horns and trampled on it, ripping the flesh almost beyond recognition.

"There's no way of telling what happened," Ysabel said, examining the horse's legs. "But it didn't bust any bones."

Which proved nothing, as he well knew. In the heat of a buffalo run, a chance false step might bring the horse down without breaking bones; and, before it could rise, the buffalo had been upon it. More than once Ysabel had seen buffalo deliberately gore and trample a fallen horse, as if seeking revenge on the animal for its part in the hunt.

"Are you sure there was a shot?" Ysabel asked.

"No," admitted Loncey. "I may have been wrong."

"None of our men has a gun along," mused Ysabel. "Maybe—"

At that moment one of the hunters galloped up. "Ysabel, there is a dispute over who killed a bull."

"I'll come."

One of the hunt leader's tasks was to keep the peace and give judgment in doubtful cases where two men both shot the same animal. Riding over to the disputed animal, Ysabel examined the arrows in its body with a view of deciding which inflicted the more serious injury. In this instance either arrow would have killed, so he insisted that the meat be divided between both men and the hide—major point of dissension—go to some *tsukup* who had no son on the hunt. Accepting their leader's decision—which pride had prevented either hunter from suggesting, lest he be thought afraid of the other—the men withdrew their arrows and waited for the arrival of the women. Ysabel found himself fully occupied with the business of butchering the kill and Loncey joined the other warriors to enjoy the perks of their labor, a feast of the usual delicacies. So the boy forgot his thoughts on the cause of the horse's death, although he wondered what he would do through the rest of the hunt.

Up on a rim overlooking the kill area, No Father saw with relief that no search had been made to discover who shot Loncey's horse. Instead of accompanying a hunting party, he had trailed along unnoticed behind Ysabel's group. On seeing Loncey take up a position on the end of the line, No Father decided to grab any opportunity to make his mother's prophecy come true. Leaving his horse, he took his rifle and cut across country until ahead of the herd. Then he found a well-concealed place and settled down to wait. Watching the rush begin, he lined his rifle and, as Loncey approached, prepared to shoot. Pure luck caused the horse to turn almost level with No Father and he had seen it fall.

Ka-Dih Himself must have been riding with the hated Loncey, for the white boy still lived.

Just a little scared at the thought of tangling with one who had such good medicine, No Father returned to his waiting horse, mounted and headed back to the camp. On his way he fell in with a party and trailed them in. If any question should be asked, he doubted if there would be proof of his presence near the Ysabel group that day.

Used to accidents and losses of horses upon buffalo hunts, Ysabel, Long Walker and Loncey gave little thought to how the animal happened to fall. By the time he returned to the camp, Loncey felt sure that he only imagined the shot and the men tended to agree with him.

Knowing she had no man for her, Loncey asked for and was granted permission to take half the meat and the whole hide of the first buffalo he killed as a gift to Raccoon Talker. The medicine woman thanked him and looked him over from head to foot.

"You have done well this day, Loncey," she said. "Aiee! I brought a fine warrior into the world the day you were born. Like all who do great deeds, you have made enemies. One in particular seeks to kill you."

"Who is it, *pia*?" asked the boy, his right hand instinctively rubbing the walnut grips of his Dragoon Colt.

"That I do not know. I feel danger for you, but no more. Your enemy has strong medicine power which prevents me from discovering his name."

Loncey did not scoff at the words. Young though he might be, the boy had seen enough of medicine men and women's power to know they possessed ways which passed beyond the understanding of ordinary people. So he took the warning seriously.

"I will watch well, *pia*," he promised.

"See you do," she replied. "If I can break the medicine power, I will speak the name of your enemy."

While Loncey took the warning seriously, he soon put it at the back of his mind. A name warrior, even on the threshold of his career, could not shiver at shadows or hide from fear of an unknown enemy. Life must go on; and if the mysterious enemy made a move, Loncey figured he carried a mighty convincing answer in his rifle, bow and arrows, Dragoon Colt or bowie knife.

As no blame could be attached to Loncey for losing the horse, he received the loan of another trained in buffalo hunting and continued to ride in his father's party. For a week or more, in all kinds of weather, he helped run down buffalo and learned the secrets of the game. No further attempts were made upon his life and he began to believe that for once Raccoon Talker made a mistake.

In actual fact No Father, scared by the medicine power which apparently saved his enemy from certain death, decided to leave further attempts until after his mother came up with some way of combating Loncey's spiritual protection.

Hard hunting caused the herds to split up and scatter, so Loncey found himself sent off on a scouting expedition. Although he saw no buffalo, he came across something almost as valuable.

While ranging some eight miles from the camp, he came upon a large herd of wild horses. Halting in cover, the boy studied the herd with particular attention given to one of its number. The majority of the herd were run-of-the-mill mustangs, smallish, wiry and tough, but nothing out of the ordinary. Not so the horse at which Loncey stared hungrily. A male just turning from colt to stallion, it must have come from high-bred stock off a ranch. Standing at least sixteen hands, the white stallion showed beauty, strength and endurance. Such an animal, if it could be taken, would make a mount that a *tuivitsi* needed to show himself to the best advantage.

Turning his mount, Loncey headed back to the camp at top speed. Once there he told his grandfather and father of his find. Always ready to increase the size of their horse herd, the two men gave permission for him to go after the

wild bunch and Ysabel promised to accompany him. All of
Loncey's young friends gathered willingly when he passed
word of his intentions. The hunting had been good, so nobody objected to the boys gaining experience in another part
of their life. Putting aside his dislike, Loncey asked No Father to accompany the party, but the boy refused.

A well-equipped party rode from the camp, each boy carrying spare food and leading three reserve horses. During
the ride to the horse herd's territory, Ysabel refreshed the
boys' memories with details of hunting and capturing wild
horses.

Possibly because of the manual labor it involved, the Comanche rarely used the corral-pen system in which the
horses were driven into a stockade of blackjack posts.
The most skilled horsemen of all the Plains Indian tribes,
the *Nemenuh* preferred more spectacular methods.

In a hard winter, when cold weather and shortage of food
made the horses gaunt and weak, men using mounts fed on
stored hay could often ride down the herd and make cap-
tures with comparative ease. Unfortunately the winter had
been mild, food plentiful and that did not apply on the current hunt.

Out on more arid country a herd might roam ten miles
from water to find decent grazing, gaining quite a thirst in
the process. By finding and ambushing the horses' watering
place, then waiting until the herd returned and drank its fill,
the hunters might dash out and collect a fair number of
mustangs busy drinking. Being in a well-watered area, such
a method would not work.

A bachelor bunch of males driven from their herds by the
dominant stallion often fell victim when the Comanches
turned a number of mares loose and swooped in while the
wild stock's attention stayed on the females. On finding the
herd to be a mixed one, Ysabel knew yet another method
could be forgotten.

So he made his plans, basing them upon the fact that a
wild horse herd tended to stick to a limited area and when

frightened ran in a rough circle around their chosen domain. Sending two of the boys to start the herd moving, Ysabel studied the escape route taken and moved the remainder of his party into what he hoped would be the center of the circle. For three days the party kept the herd moving, allowing it time to neither rest, sleep satisfactorily nor drink in peace. Always two or three of the boys would be on hand, relaying their mounts and changing with the next section to take up the pursuit. Riding on the inside of the herd's territorial circle, the boys covered less distance and had the advantage that their mounts could do all the things they prevented the herd from doing.

At last Ysabel decided the moment had come to make the capture. Each boy took the horse that he had not used and kept fresh, shook the coils from his lariat, and headed for the herd. Charging down on the leg-weary, exhausted horses, the boys snaked out the pick of them.

While most of the boys carried two or three ropes, wishing to take as many horses as possible, Loncey had eyes for only one animal. Mounted on a bay noted for its speed, he headed straight for the white stallion. Exhausted it might be, but the stallion turned and ran. For a time Loncey feared that the bay would be left behind, so fast did the white run, but at last the strain of the continuous hazing told. Even so the white ran until it could go no more. Coming up as the lathered white stood with hanging head, Loncey sent his rope flickering out. Even as the noose closed about the white's neck, he bounded from the bay and started up the rope toward his capture. A snort left the white's lips and it tried to attack. Like a living thing, the rope in Loncey's hands coiled around the white's forelegs and brought it down.

Already exhausted, the white stallion could not rise and lay on the ground while the boy came toward it. Swiftly he pulled out the so-called "wild" hairs from around the white's eyes, fixed the rope hackamore about its head and then blew into its flaring nostrils.

After supervising the other boys, Ysabel collected a gentle mare from the rough camp he and the boys had been using, then rode after his son. He came on the scene just as the white made its feet. One look told Ysabel why Loncey did not try to gather in more than the one horse.

"That's a real fine-looking hoss, boy," he said admiringly.

"And I caught him, *'ap*," Loncey replied. Under Comanche law, the person who captured a wild horse claimed it for his own.

"You caught him all right," Ysabel agreed, studying the defiance in the exhausted horse's manner. "Now all you've got to do is tame him down, break and train him."

"I aim to do just that," Loncey stated.

"See you made a start," remarked his father admiringly. "Now let's get him hitched to the mare while we still can."

Having seen an example of the stallion's spirit, Loncey heartily agreed with his father. Quickly they took a length of rope and secured the white to the mare, leaving enough play on the connection for her to be able to avoid injury during the stallion's struggles for freedom. Having often been used for such work, the mare knew what she must do and avoided the stallion's bites and kicks while preventing it from charging the human beings.

In a short time the white realized the futility of trying to run away, dragging the mare behind it. However, it would not permit Loncey to approach and showed plainly that any attempt would most likely prove dangerous if not fatal. Loncey did not mind. Time was on his side and he could play the waiting game. Crossing to his waiting horse, he swung astride it and joined his father. Followed by the mare and reluctant white, the two humans rode back to the temporary camp. While the white drank at a small stream, the other boys gathered around and muttered their admiration at the sight of it.

All in all the hunt had been a success. Every Indian boy managed to take at least two mustangs and Comes For Food gathered in four, after grabbing a rope from the hands of a companion who appeared content to have two captives on his hands. For all their multiple successes, none of the boys thought less of Loncey's only taking one horse. They knew quality when they saw it and recognized that the white stallion, properly broken and trained, would be the equal of three or four ordinary broomtailed mustangs.

"We'll go back to the buffalo camp," Ysabel ordered, glancing up at the sky. "There's still work to be done on these horses."

Unless being selected as suitable for breeding, or intended as a favorite mount, male horses were castrated. A gelding caused less trouble in the remuda than a stallion would and proved easier to handle. So, on arrival at the buffalo-hunt camp, the boys selected their best horse and went to work on the others. Roping the horse's forelegs, they brought it down and tied its feet to a post. Two of the boys laid hold of the hind legs and a third, watched over by Ysabel, handled the knife. Working deftly and swiftly, the boy performed the operation. So efficient had been their training that not one horse was lost or seriously injured during the gelding.

Naturally Loncey did not subject the white stallion to that treatment. Wishing to make the white a one-man horse, he requested permission to return to the village. Always willing to encourage initiative, the leaders of the hunt allowed him to go. Accompanied by four of his friends, he rode back to the main village, but did not settle there. A *tsukup* wise in such matters taught the boys how to set up a pole corral. Building one close to a deep water hole a mile from the village, aided by his friends, Loncey placed the white stallion and mare inside. Then he had a tepee erected and stayed there alone.

For a week the boy could not approach the stallion. Each day he gathered such titbits as might tempt the horse's fancy, spending every possible minute near it. At last his persistence won through and the stallion began to allow him close, then to touch, fondle and caress its sleek skin. Freed from the mare, the white showed no sign of trying to run and Loncey went on with the next stage of training.

By the time the buffalo hunters returned, laden with a winter-long supply of meat, hides and all the other parts used in their lives, Loncey had taught the stallion to come when he whistled or called, and to accept the feel of blanket, then saddle, on its back.

Everything the boy saw warned him that putting on the saddle would be easier than persuading the white to accept him as a rider. So he started to lead the horse to the water hole and wade out until the water lapped around its belly. Regarding this as a pleasant sensation, the big white went in willingly and Loncey carefully checked the bottom. He found only firm sand, no rocks on which the horse might damage a leg, so knew he could put the next step of the training into operation.

Leading the horse into the water as usual, Loncey fastened a rope securely to his saddle, knotting the other end firmly about his waist. Then he slowly levered himself onto the horse's back. Feeling the unaccustomed weight, the white began to rear in an effort to dislodge whatever might be on its back. Deftly Loncey kept its head down and it started to buck. Even impeded by the water, the white put such fury into its efforts that it threw Loncey. He came up spluttering, grabbing the rope in both hands and halting the horse's rush for the shore. Three more times the white threw Loncey and he swung back astride on rising. At last the boy's tenacity won out; he kept in the saddle and rode the horse to a standstill. When the horse fought no more, Loncey led it from the water and back to the corral.

From that day Loncey continued to ride the stallion, sitting out its bucking until it understood that it could not throw him. Kindness and patience kept the stallion from losing its spirit even though it no longer fought against carrying him on its back. Not until the fighting ended did Loncey cease to fasten himself in the saddle.

The work of training did not end with being able to ride

the white, it was only the beginning. A Comanche's favorite horse must be more than a mere means to take one from place to place. It had to be obedient to various commands and able to act as an extra pair of eyes and ears, and a spare nose, for its master.

Aided by his friends, Loncey taught the horse to locate and give warning of hidden men, a simple task as the horse retained most of its wild instincts. The boy watched and studied its reactions, learning to read every head toss, snort or ear twitch. Observing from a distance, Ysabel and Long Walker nodded their approval and repeatedly told each other that they had never seen such a horse before.

Others also observed Loncey's activities, but with less innocent intent. Fire Dancer watched and an idea began to form in her head. Due to Ysabel's previous caution, she had not achieved anything in the way of revenge. At last she saw a chance to strike at the big white man through his son.

"If you go against *Cuchillo* while he is out there with the horse," she told No Father, "you could kill him and none will know who did it. If you take the horse they will blame the Waco, or Apaches."

"I could take my rifle—" the boy began.

"You missed the last time you tried that. There is another way."

"You mean go after him with a knife—*alone*?" asked No Father, showing a remarkable lack of enthusiasm.

"Not alone. Have you no friends?"

"Some, but they will not kill another member of the People."

"How about the captive boys?"

Recently No Father had befriended five boys captured in raids on different Indian tribes. With his mother's help in the way of food, he turned them into willing cronies. However, No Father was unsure of how much sway he had over them.

"I don't know—"

"Go and speak with them, bring them here," ordered his mother. "We will see."

Gathering the captive boys, No Father brought them to his mother's tepee and she spoke to them of her medicine. To hear Fire Dancer tell it, the boys could be made free and returned to their own people—with her aid—if they helped kill the one called *Cuchillo*. Although the prospect of freedom might be alluring, one of the boys, a bulky, tall Tejas, raised objections.

"If we kill a *Tshaoh*, they will kill us."

"First they must catch you," Fire Dancer pointed out.

"A horse can run faster than a mule," countered the Tejas.

The Comanche never allowed captives to ride other than mules, which lacked the speed to escape from pursuing horses.

"I have horses for you. There will be a storm tomorrow, its rain will hide your tracks as you flee. But you must help No Father kill *Cuchillo* or my medicine will ensure your capture."

"*Cuchillo* has weapons," objected the Tejas.

"So will you," promised Fire Dancer and walked to her bed. Drawing aside the buffalo robe blanket, she exposed a collection of knives and tomahawks. "There. Come to me in the early hours of the morning and I will arm you. Then you go with No Father, kill *Cuchillo* and ride to freedom."

"And if we don't?" the Tejas inquired.

"You remember the *Kweharehnuh* who died in this camp many seasons ago?" hissed Fire Dancer and the boys nodded. "My medicine killed him because he would not obey me. Now what do you say?"

"We go with No Father," answered the scared Tejas while his companions gave their agreement.

In the early gray light of the morning Raccoon Talker left her tepee and walked hurriedly through the camp. Although headed for the home of Long Walker and Ysabel, she halted on seeing two young shapes approaching. On their way home after a night at playing stealing horses, Comes For Food—renamed Four Horses due to his exploit on the mustang hunt—and Loud Voice halted at the woman's low spoken command.

"I smell evil in the air," she told the boys. "Danger threatens *Cuchillo*—"

The boys needed to hear no more. Even when playing their inevitable horse-stealing game, they carried their knives. So, without waiting to collect other weapons, they ran to collect horses so as to reach their friend the more quickly. After watching the boys go, Raccoon Talker turned and hurried on to her original destination.

16

A Chance to Ride to War

While it had not been No Father's original intention to accompany the captive boys on the actual attack, they stood firm in their refusal to go without him. So, rather than put aside what might be the best chance they would ever have to kill Loncey, Fire Dancer insisted that her son go along. He alone of the party possessed a firearm. In addition to his rifle, a Colt 1851 Navy revolver rode in his waist belt. Although wanting revenge, Fire Dancer did not dare advertise her intentions by obtaining bows and arrows, so the remainder of the raiding force bore either knives or tomahawks.

Scattered around Loncey's tepee, the boys made their cautious way through the cold gray light of the dawn. Overhead, sullen black clouds gave warning spatters of rain, but as yet the full force of the impending storm had not broken. The Tejas, smarter and less trusting than the others, saw numerous snags in the proposed murder and horse theft. After its success, he doubted whether Fire Dancer would allow the party to go free. So he decided to act for himself. Leaving the others to stalk Loncey's tepee, he made a cautious way toward the gate of the corral. In doing so, he alerted and warned the white stallion.

In the tepee Loncey came from deep sleep to full awake at the horse's first alarmed snort. Automatically he scooped up the revolver in his right hand and bowie knife in his left. Rising, he paused and listened to the scraping of the corral's gate pole. No Comanche boy would play at horse stealing so far from the camp and with the animal another of the People kept penned for private training. That meant somebody made a serious attempt to steal the white stallion. Letting out a low hiss of anger, Loncey burst through the tepee's door.

A shape loomed ahead of him, coming with upraised knife. Already cocked on being taken up, the Dragoon boomed. Struck in the chest by the soft lead ball, the first attacker went over backward. At Loncey's right, a second boy hurled his tomahawk. Lack of skill caused the head of the handle to strike instead of the blade, but it hit Loncey's right wrist with numbing force and caused him to let the heavy Dragoon fall from limp fingers.

Letting out a screech, the tomahawk thrower hurled at Loncey with bare hands. Pivoting, Loncey brought up his knife in a savage backhand slash over the reaching arms and laid the other boy's throat open to the bone. Even as he struck, Loncey saw enough to tell him what had been planned.

Down by the corral, the Tejas boy let the top gate pole fall and vaulted over it. Unless he sadly misjudged, the white could clear the lower poles even carrying him, so he did not need to waste further time. Starting forward, he heard the stallion snort, saw its ears flatten—then it charged him. Before the boy could decide on what action to take, the stallion reached him. Rearing high, the white slashed out with its hooves and drove them into the boy's skull. Although the Tejas crashed down with his skull smashed open, the stallion

did not halt its attack. Screaming with fighting rage, it
stamped the body into a bloody pulp.

Loncey saw No Father rise from behind a bush and start
to bring up the rifle. At the same moment, a third boy, a
Waco, rushed up and presented more immediate danger to
Loncey's life. Like most Indians, the Waco held his knife
with the blade beneath his hand in a way which allowed
only two types of blow: a downward chop aimed behind his
enemy's collarbone, or a sideways stroke directed to the ribs.
The Waco elected to try the former attack and brought the
knife swinging downward. Before Waco steel could blood
itself in his flesh, Loncey threw up his numb right forearm
to block the other's knife wrist. Then the bowie knife gave
its answer; only Loncey held it as taught by Don Francisco
Almonte, its blade extending from the thumb and forefinger
side of the hand. Such a grip allowed the knife to be used for
its most deadly stroke, the driving, ripping cross-slash.
Holding off the Waco's knife, Loncey sank the bowie's blade
into the other's belly and tore it open.

Hooves thundered and drew No Father's attention from
Loncey. Seeing Loud Voice and Comes For Food tearing
down to the rescue, and noting they were closer to him than
Loncey, No Father swung his rifle toward them. He aimed
and fired, driving a .56 caliber bullet into Loud Voice's head
and tumbling him from the back of the racing pony. Tossing
aside the empty rifle, No Father started to draw the Navy
Colt. Not so brave as the others, the remaining captive boy
had advanced less speedily and found himself in the path of
Comes For Food's horse. With the courage of a cornered rat,
the captive hurled himself forward. Comes For Food
whipped out his knife and dived from his horse onto his
attacker, both of them crashing to the ground.

Giving a roar of rage, Loncey charged at No Father to
avenge the killing of his foster brother. The Colt swung his
way and he went forward in a rolling dive. He heard the
crash of the shot and felt a searing, burning pain on his
shoulder, while being half-blinded by the Colt's muzzle

blast. Seeing Loncey coming, No Father started to spring aside. Loncey slashed viciously sideways in passing. The knife sliced into No Father's calf so deep that it tore through the muscles almost to the bone. Blood spurted and No Father gave a scream, staggering and dropping the revolver.

On hearing the first shot and seeing the arrival of the two *Pehnane* boys, Fire Dancer realized that her plan might fail and help was sure to come from the village. Leading her son's horse, she charged out from where she had been hiding and raced toward No Father. Comes For Food rose from disposing of the boy he tackled, heard the drumming of hooves and whirled to deal with the newcomer should he prove to be an enemy. Recognizing Fire Dancer, the boy paused, undecided as to what he ought to do. Fire Dancer pulled the single-shot pistol from her waistband, lining it and firing. Lead ripped into Comes For Food's chest, spun him around and tumbled him aside.

At that point Fire Dancer saw her son receive the injury and screamed in rage. There was no way she could reload the pistol and she possessed no other means of dealing with Loncey. Already in the distance she could see two men galloping toward the battleground and recognized them. With Ysabel and Long Walker coming, she dare waste no time. Showing riding skill of a high order, she tore down and scooped her son onto the horse in passing. Give him his due, hurt badly though he might be, No Father still retained the presence of mind to catch his mother's wrist and swing afork the horse behind her. Before Loncey could rise, the horses whirled by and tore away. Wild with rage, he caught up No Father's heavy Navy Colt, but could not make a hit on the fast riding, double-loaded couple. Turning, Loncey dashed to the corral, meaning to use his white for the pursuit. Hot with fury still, it showed obvious signs that warned Loncey that to enter the corral at that moment would be suicide.

Rain began to come down faster, lightning flashed and

thunder rolled. Before Ysabel and Long Walker arrived, the storm broke in all its fury.

"Who was it, boy?" demanded Ysabel, leaping from the grulla as it slid to a halt at his son's side.

"Fire Dancer and No Father," Loncey answered. "Let me have your horse, *'ap.*"

"Loud Voice is dead!" Long Walker called from by the boy's body.

"Give me the horse, *'ap!*" Loncey repeated.

"You couldn't find them in this storm, boy," Ysabel answered gently. "And you've got a mighty bad gash on your back."

Not until that moment did Loncey realize he had been wounded. Before allowing himself to be taken to the village for treatment, he insisted on replacing the corral rail so as to keep the white stallion inside.

The following afternoon Loncey stood in his grandfather's tepee, facing the chief, Ysabel, War Club and Comes For Food's father—the latter two haggard with grief at the loss of their sons. After he told of the attack, Loncey stated his intention of finding Fire Dancer and her son even though the storm wiped out their tracks.

"I had old Buffalo Keates come in to see me the other day, boy," Ysabel interrupted. "Was fixing to tell you when you could handle the white. The South's gone to war with the Yankees and Texas is siding with the Confederate States, which being what the southern states call themselves. Buffalo said that Mosby gent we showed some buffalo hunting a couple of years back wants us to go along and join a regiment he's starting to fight the Yankees."

"You mean to ride to war?" Loncey gasped.

"Sure, boy."

For a long time the boy stood without a word. At last he could achieve every Comanche boy's ambition of taking the war trail. But if he did, he must put off his vengeance search for No Father.

"We will understand if you go, my son," War Club told

the boy and Comes For Food's father nodded agreement. A war trail of that kind took precedence over the quest for vengeance and any other business.

"*Ka-Dih* does not favor you hunting them at this time, *tawk*," Long Walker went on. "That was why he sent the storm to wash out their tracks. Ride to war and count many coups."

"Very well, *tawk*," Loncey said quietly. "I will. I will come back, find No Father—and when I do, one of us will die."

How Loncey finally met No Father and kept his promise is told in *Sidewinder*.